MATTHEW RATTON

The fire at Flint Hill farm ruined more than Matthew Ratton's livelihood. It disfigured his face cruelly and transformed him into a suspicious recluse. Nothing further remained in his life outside his bankrupt sheep farm; but he reckoned without a weak, blind, half-dead collie pup called Jet who is taken home by Matthew to be fed, tended and trained, as his sheep dog. Matthew slowly returns to the world around him; his farm, the countryside and Mary West and, with Jet beside him, begins to work with a new determination.

MATTHEW RATTON

Matthew Ratton

by
Anne Knowles

MAGNA PRINT BOOKS
Long Preston, Yorkshire,
England.

British Library Cataloguing in Publication Data

Knowles, Anne
 Matthew Ratton.—Large print ed.
 I. Title
 823'.914(F)   PR6061.N547

 ISBN 0-86009-438-3

First Published in Great Britain by Eyre Methuen Ltd 1980

Copyright © 1980 by Anne Knowles

Published in Large Print 1982 by arrangement with Eyre Methuen
Ltd London and St Martins' Press Inc. New York

Photoset in Great Britain by
Dermar Phototypesetting Co. Long Preston, Yorkshire.

Printed in Great Britain by
Redwood Burn Limited, Trowbridge, Wiltshire and
bound by Pegasus Bookbinding, Melksham, Wiltshire.

CHAPTER 1

He knew it was a dream, but his mind would not let him waken. He was dreaming as a dog dreams: his muscles twitching to the stimulus of his brain, his frame agitated by phantoms. It would have distressed anyone watching, had there been anyone there to watch, but to have touched him to wake him would have brought scant thanks. He was not a man to accept help gladly.

He could feel an intensity of heat round him. He was in the fire again, with the stink of smoke in his nostrils, and the terrible roar and crack of burning timbers. He felt eyebrows and hair shrivelling and singeing, and his throat was hot and dry. Trig was here, somewhere, if only he could find her. Three times she had gone back into the cowhouse to get the old girls out of danger, but the third time he had heard her yelp and howl and he knew she must be trapped. Best bitch in the world, she was. Clever as a Christian. Cunning as a cat. There's not many will herd sheep and drive dairy cows: chivvying the one, patiently guiding the other, matching mood with the creatures in their charge, but Trig could. She could pen a bull, or a brood of day-old chicks, with a skill you'd be hard put to believe if you hadn't seen it. Matthew could see her now. She was caught by the leg where a beam lay smouldering. He called out and ran to her. Above her the roof crackled and roared, and she lay under the glare of it, waiting for him, not struggling, knowing he would fetch her out. The beam that trapped her seared his hands, but he was so driven by anger and fear that he felt nothing. Her coat was harsh with the heat as he took her up and turned to the doorway. The noise of the roof as it fell shocked him out of sleep and he lay sweating and shivering, and the scars on his face pulled down from eye and mouth as they did when he was afraid and the muscles twitched in his cheek.

He was used to this nightmare now. Whenever he woke, haunted by it, he would force his memory to bring back to him every detail of the day of the fire: the hot, heavy August air, parched with drought; everyone glad of the least patch of shade to keep off the oppressive sun. There had never been less rainfall in all the summers Matthew could remember, even when he was a child and the memory of summer was all sunshine. Stream-beds were dry, and the hydraulic ram that pumped water to house and fields fell silent as even the deep springs that fed it trickled to nothing. Only the slimy, echoing well in the yard was left to provide them with precious water for themselves and the stock, and they had carried bucketsful until their arms seemed loosened from their shoulders. It had made for a good cereal crop, well ripened and dry, though there was not much cereal grown at Flint Hill. Sheep grazed the higher pastures, and cattle the rich meadows of the valley bottom. There was good hay off these meadows too, but only occasionally was a field put down to barley or wheat. It was left to Pennant Farm, lower down the valley, with its wider fields open all day to the sun, to grow grain for winter feed, and Matthew and his father had been down there helping with the harvest. The Daveys at Pennant had been their neighbours for a good many years, and they gave each other a hand, turn and turn about, whenever work on the farms demanded it.

It must have been the hottest day of that hot summer, and they had been shifting bales in the thirty-acre while John Davey drove the combine in the next field. The wheat stalks scratched great red weals on dry skin, and the chaffy, seedless heads crept into the clothing and itched intolerably. Everyone was weary and short-tempered with the heat.

Jim and Michael Alderton, two young lads from Shepley, were helping stack the bales on the trailer. It was hard work, especially when the load was piled high, and Dan Ratton was looking sour at the job they had made of it, and giving them the rough edge of his tongue.

'You'll lose the whole bloody lot before you reach the field's edge. Why can't you load it properly?'

'It'll be OK, Mr Ratton,' the bolder of the two, young Mike, had said, intent on saving himself the work of reloading.

'Like hell it will,' the old man had bawled, and seizing a bale that was poised ready to topple, had thrown it towards Mike with such force that it had carried itself and a couple of others over the side to hit the stubble, burst their twine and scatter straw everywhere.

'That'll be out of your wages!' the old man had shouted, and moved forward, taking breath as he did so to give the boys a further piece of his mind.

It was one of the still pictures that was imprinted on Matthew's memory: the angry old man and the sullen young one, about to move forward, to come to blows perhaps, on the piled straw-bales that glittered whitely against the intense blue sky. They never made that angry move, though, for as he looked beyond Mike, across the stubble to where Flint Hill Farm stood, Dan Ratton had seen the first smoke-shimmer, only for a fraction of a second allowed himself to hope it was heat-haze, and then had recognized on the still air the bitter-sweet smell of burning hay. He had let out a shout that stopped every man in the field where he stood, and in moments they were all making for Flint Hill as fast as they could, leaving the harvest fields deserted, bales all dropped askew, a row of wheat half cut, and the combine, like some defunct monster, squatting silent on the stubble it had made.

John Davey had stopped off at Pennant to phone for the fire brigade, and Matthew and his father and the other men took one look at the flames leaping from the hay barn and buckled down to the hopeless, sweating, despairing process of fetching water up from the well to fight the blaze.

The end wall of the cowhouse abutted the haybarn and flames had already caught the roof timbers. In any other summer the building would have been empty at this time of day, with the dairy cows out to pasture, but their grazing was dry and scorched and the flies such a torment to them in the heat that they had been left in the cowhouse to browse on hay in the cool shade of the thick-walled building. Trig had not needed to be told to fetch them out. She knew, as if by instinct, the danger they were in and within minutes she had the first couple blundering out into the yard, shaking their heads, bewildered and confused, their placid lives disrupted by this terrible thing that was happening.

Matthew had left her to it, knowing the dog could be trusted. It was only when he heard the clamour of the fire engine that he was able to pause for a moment from the muscle-tearing pull and heave and swing of the water-buckets.

'Where's your supply, mate?' a fireman shouted, and Matthew pointed to the well.

'Any left down there?'

'Yes,' said Matthew, though it seemed to him a whole ocean could not quell the blaze from the burning hay.

'Let's get on with it then.'

It was as he helped the man reel hose down into the depths that he heard Trig howl.

Matthew stared at the ceiling, wondering whether this dream would ever leave him. It was a recurrent horror to him, though he had learned to control the shaking and sweating into which he always woke by this deliberate recollection. It was a ritual, this exact remembering of events, like the rituals with which a child will comfort itself on its way to bed up a long, dark stair.

Soon it would be time to get up for milking. He had been doing that job since he was old enough to carry a bucket, and that was coming up for thirty years. God, how he had had to run, those mornings when he was at school in Clipton. As soon as the last cow left the shed, he would push a few mouthfuls of breakfast down himself and take off down the track to where the bus pulled up at the junction with the Clipton road. Dan Ratton had made sure his sons earned their keep all right. David was to have the farm, of course, being the elder, but that was no reason to let Matthew off. Once he had started at Clipton Grammar though, and there was homework to be done, it made a day long enough to be daunting, and sometimes he would be in trouble for dozing off in class. He thought about Miss Atherly, the teacher at the village school in Shepley. What a woman she was: the bright, clear mind of her, and the way she had persuaded old man Ratton that the world would not collapse if he sent Matthew on to the Grammar School.

Jane Atherly had gone to school with Matthew's mother, Hannah Black, as she was then, and Miss Atherly saw that Matthew had inherited his mother's intelligence, and a good deal of her ability, which Dan Ratton set no value on at all. In Miss Atherly's opinion it was a waste of a life, Hannah marrying Dan Ratton. She had died when Matthew was hardly more than a baby. David Ratton was his father all over again, but in Matthew Jane Atherly saw promise that she was determined to encourage. She made sure that Matthew was allowed to keep all his mother's books, and the folders full of her delicate drawings of wildlife, and her detailed accounts of the creatures she had seen in the countryside round Shepley. They would have gone on the bonfire if the old man had had his way.

So Matthew knew, almost by heart, books like Gilbert White's *Natural History of Selbourne* and Richard Jefferies' *The Life of the Fields*. Encouraged further by Jane Atherly, he had discovered his own ability to draw, and she developed in him an orderly, careful, retentive mind and an observant, compassionate eye. His drawings of plants were exact in every detail and his knowledge of them grew with observation, yet they were always more than mere botanical studies. To Dan Ratton it seemed womanish to be interested in such things, yet everything about Matthew as he grew up belied this and set Dan's mind at rest, though he grumbled all the same. Big-framed and with broad, competent hands, Matthew was as deft with an axe as with a pencil. Dan saw, with something approaching pride, how little Patty James, the dentist's daughter, ogled after Matthew when he first went to the Clipton school. She would not take long in teaching him what girls were for. True enough, it was with Patty that Matthew had played his first love-games, and on one warm spring evening, when David had taunted Matthew because he was busy drawing when David wanted help to snare rabbits—he had called him a stupid girl and Matthew had bloodied his nose for him—it was Patty who had more than willingly allowed him to prove he was nothing of the sort.

Gradually, as he grew up, it became established in Matthew's mind that he would make some good use of the knowledge he was acquiring at school: would move on, away from Flint Hill and from Shepley, into a wider world. What he wanted to do he was not himself sure, though the school talked in terms of university, a degree perhaps. They certainly thought him more than capable. Then one day, when Matthew was a few weeks off his seventeenth birthday, David was out harrowing the steep meadow behind the house and overturned the tractor. He died instantly.

When the two of them had been small boys at Sunday school, the rector had privately referred to Matthew and David as Jacob and Esau. They were about as dissimilar, but Matthew had none of Jacob's cunning, and no brother ever had a birthright thrust upon him that was was so unwilling to accept. There was no arguing with Dan Ratton though. Once he had weathered his grief at David's death, he made it quite clear that his indulgence to Matthew in the matter of school was finished. He must leave at once and work Flint Hill alongside his father, as David had done since he had left school at sixteen. The farm would be his now, and his first duty must be towards the land. Matthew had surprised himself to find how much he resented this. He had always loved Flint Hill—it had been the background of his life, the colour and the music of it, the changing seasons in field and wood—but he had looked out to wider horizons, had, in his mind, packed for a more demanding journey, and he did not wish to stay merely to suit his father's purpose, to be a poor substitute for David.

Dan Ratton did not find it easy, either, to accept this odd second-best that fate had handed him. 'I don't suppose I'll understand you if I live a hundred years, he would say. 'Will it get your fields ploughed any quicker or your crop better sown that you've sat up half the night drawing flowers and such? And as for the wild things you make such a fuss about, they're half of them enemies that'll rob you of your living if you don't watch out.'

Matthew would bite back the answers that he knew might convince someone of a more open mind. He had learned there was no use talking to his father about natural balance, about the importance of proportion. To Dan Ratton all hawks should be shot, all foxes poisoned, all wild flowers should be labelled weeds and kept as far as possible out of his pastures. Matthew kept quiet, kept to his own beliefs, and went his own way.

He went to see Miss Atherly. He had had her ear for all his problems for as long as he could remember. He had gone to her even when he was quite tiny to clear and soothe his mind, as he had gone to Pennant to the comfort of Peggy Davey when he was hurt or hungry.

Miss Atherly felt angry at Dan Ratton's decision, but she did not show it. She was bitterly disappointed for Matthew, and a little for herself too, for she had longed to see the promise in him properly kept, but what could she say? Dan had lost his elder son, the good, practical, down-to-earth farmer. Miss Atherly's private opinion was that David Ratton was a clod, but the poor lad was dead now, and no point speaking ill of him. Matthew could do the work all right, he had the practical ability, but what a shameful waste to harness a high-flyer to the plough. Half afraid that he would feel she was in some way betraying him to just this fate, she said, 'Matthew, unless you want to break away entirely from your father and from this place, you will have to make up your mind to accept certain things as they are.'

'I suppose so,' Matthew said, dully. 'I don't want to let Dad down, but I did want to be something different. Something more. The trouble is I don't even really know what. I suppose if I had some great calling, to be a doctor, or a zoologist, or a priest, even, that would make up my mind for me and nothing would stop me doing it: not my father, not the farm, and not Shepley either.'

Miss Atherly looked sharply at him. 'You are very astute, even in disappointment,' she said. 'You were well on the way to discovering yourself, and now circumstances have blown up the road for you, if you will allow a somewhat violent metaphor. Now I shall give you some advice which you may find extremely trite, in which case you are at liberty to ignore it. Take the job on, Matthew, and use everything you have learned to make a success of it. Your father is a cussed old man, and I am one of his generation and allowed to say it, but you will find you can learn a good deal from him too. You can be a farmer without being a brainless peasant. Farming is a skill, a craft. Take a pride in it. Your father is no fool, despite his shortcomings, so let him teach you his mysteries as I have tried to teach you mine.'

'I suppose I must,' Matthew said.

'One more thing,' Miss Atherly went on. 'Accept these things, as I said, but don't let yourself become entirely buried

in practicalities. Hold on to the awareness you have now of the whole pattern
of life, and don't be ashamed of the
beauty to be found in it. Look for it consciously. Make yourself look for it. And
above all, never feel that anything you
have ever learned has been wasted, that
anything you have ever drawn or
observed or written about could have
been time better spent, though a good
many people may try to persuade you
otherwise.'

Matthew had taken her advice: he had
done his best, despite the constant
clashes in temperament between himself
and his father, determined to prove to
himself that his opportunities had not
been lost, only re-shaped. At times it had
been difficult in the extreme. He remembered how Patty James had gone off a
couple of years later to Bristol University, and was to be seen from time to
time with various gaudy young men with
braying voices. On the rare occasions
that she and Matthew met, she made him
feel like a turnip head. Once he had tried

to make love to her, and she had been willing enough, and so had he, until he saw that look of supreme condescension in her eye, as if he were some earthy thing out of a Lawrence novel, an Experience, to be had for the asking, and no doubt for the telling when she rejoined her college friends. He had turned away from her, furious and frustrated, and when she had come after him, he had taken her by the shoulders and shaken her until she screamed and ran, terrified by this unexpected violence.

It was the day after that Matthew had gone to Clipton market and had been offered a good sheepdog pup by a little Welshman he sometimes met in the pub there. He had come home with her stuffed unceremoniously into his coat pocket, her black head with its white triangular blaze looking out on the world with great surprise. He had devoted every spare moment to her and in the end had her trained so well that even Dan Ratton could not fault her. So he had his Trig, and he had his work, and sometimes he would walk out with a pretty, gentle girl from Brierton, who made no demands on him and made him feel good. She had been a fair little wisp of a lass, so shy she had hardly raised her eyes to him the first time they went out together. He had liked that: liked the delicate movements she made, and the way she listened so quiet and attentive when he told her of his plans. She had been married several years now to the son of the newsagent in Clipton, who was every bit as shy. People used to say he had written out his proposal and put it in with the newspapers as they did with notices about jumble sales and village meetings. Still, they had had three children, one after another, so they must have got over their shyness somehow. She had been a dear little lass. What was her name? Rose? Rosa? Matthew could not remember. He had grown out of her, grown away from her, and had become too busy to replace her. The farm demanded all the time he could give it. He did not forget Miss Atherly's advice over the years, though, and she did not let him forget it, demanding to see, whenever they met, his latest drawings, his latest field studies. Even over these he fell foul of his father, though, when he wished to leave shelter and cover for wild creatures in hedgerow and copse; when he insisted on replanting blackthorn when most of their neighbours were grubbing it out; when he would not agree to piping away the Littlebrook stream for irrigation because the dippers bred by the broken water where the stream came over the rocks. He was of age now, though, and a full partner. His father had agreed to this when Matthew had first left school as a step in Matthew's direction, not realizing how forcibly the boy would put his own opinions when the time came.

Well, with his father dead, the farm belonged to Matthew now, or what was left of it. Burned, damned near bankrupted. Which do I mean, Matthew wondered, as he swung his legs out of bed. The farm, or me?

He walked across the room and looked at himself in the mirror in the pale early light. A crack ran down the length of it, but it did to shave in, even though it showed an asymmetric image. But then his face was an asymmetric image too. Less work to shave half a face. Scar tissue does not produce much beard.

He continued to consider his face in the lop-sided glass. The undamaged side, dark-haired, dark-eyed, would look very much the same for the next twenty years, with luck. The Rattons aged slowly: the brisk air of their livelihood tanned the skin and preserved it against all weathers, and their hair retained its colour. Above the scars, though, on the left side, Matthew's hair was white.

'You look like a miscegenated badger,' he told himself.

The opalescent tissue on the scarred side had long ceased to shock him, and he had grown used to the tightness of skin by his left eyelid. He could live with it, but he asked no one else to. Since the fire he had felt old: not old in years, but old as a stone is old, with no feeling, no lust in him. It was a kind of contentment, he supposed, to want no pity, no comment, no concessions, and to realize of a surety that the only person from whom he could expect such a deal was himself.

He shrugged himself into his clothes, and went out into the yard to bring in the cows.

CHAPTER 2

That evening, down the hill at Pennant Farm, John Davey's collie bitch, Mag, lay on a bed of sacks by the kitchen fire. Now and then she would get up, restless, and scratch at her bedding or look up at her master with reproach. She had done nothing wrong, but there was pain in her belly and she felt miserable. Once, when she was a pup, she had stolen food from the table and John Davey had not only given her a beating, he had laid a trap for her of meat laced with pepper and castor oil, so that she retched and burned for hours. This pain was different, but it would not leave her alone.

'How's she doing, John?' Peggy Davey called from upstairs.

'Making heavy weather of it. I don't think she knows what it's all about.'

'Well, that's not to be wondered at.

She's not had pups before. Shall I come down and sit with her?'

'No, you get off to sleep, love. I'll wait a while down here with her.'

The fire stirred and settled. All the lamps were out but the one on the kitchen table, and all the household was quiet, except for the quick panting of the dog, and the wheezing of John Davey's pipe. The mice, circumspect, kept to their holes. There was no point in courting trouble.

John must had drifted off to sleep, for he was suddenly aware of the unmistakable noise of puppies being washed and generally attended to. Mag, utterly surprised for a moment by these odd creatures that had arrived from inside her, had then, overcome by the practicality of instinct, set about making them clean and tidy. They had put her to a good deal of trouble and discomfort. At least she would make sure that they were a credit to her.

'Well now, that's a clever lass,' her master said, and she let her tail stir slightly, but wary of him for all that, not quite sure whether this odd thing that had happened to her was acceptable to humans or not. Besides, she was not entirely sure that she wanted the puppies touched.

John made no attempt to touch them, though, but went to fetch her a bowl of hot milk with something strange and spiritous in it that made her sneeze, but after it she felt pleasantly warm and drowsy. Only then did John upturn the pups, and discover two dogs and a bitch, strong, healthy and nicely marked: one almost the image of Mag, who was named after her markings which were like a magpie's.

'You've done well for a first time,' John praised her. 'I'll tidy you up a bit, and then we'll get some sleep, or it will be tomorrow before we've finished today.'

When he had gone, Mag curled up in a crescent round her puppies, head on paws, half-dozing, half-awake, and feeling pleased with herself. Her offspring had crawled to the food-source and gorged themselves, and having suffered a further washing, had all fallen asleep.

Then, unexpectedly, that pain that she had already forgotten gripped her once more, and she yelped and looked in surprise at her flanks. Then it came again, and suddenly there was another puppy, small and still, in its sticky covering. She licked it, but wearily, without much enthusiasm, and was almost immediately asleep.

The pup lay still for a while, and then, lifting its blind head, it began to make its way to Mag's flank. The effort exhausted it, but it got there, and took a mouthful or so of milk with its remaining energy. It fell asleep then and when it woke again at first light the others were awake too and jostled it out of the way. Mag looked at it without much interest. She had her three fine babies. That was enough.

Peggy was down first and called up to John Davey that Mag had had a fourth puppy.

'It's a bitch, John. She doesn't look too strong.'

By the time the early morning jobs had been done it was obvious that Mag had rejected the puppy. She lay where her brothers and sister had shoved her, cold and barely moving. Peggy held her to Mag's teats, but she had little energy to suck and Mag soon nosed her away.

'Don't bother with it, Peggy. The bitch knows best. If she won't nurse it, there's more than likely something wrong with it. Midday, when I come in, I'll do away with it.'

Peggy hated to see the little thing lying there so forlorn, though, and she made a hot bottle for her and tucked her up in an old grocery box, and put it near the fire, but by midday the pup lay unmoving and quiet as death.

'Well, it's saved me the job,' John Davey said. 'Sorry, Peggy love, but the pup's dead. I'll put it outside and bury it later. You content yourself with the three we've got. Look, Mag's happy enough.'

Mag pricked her ears at the mention of

her name and her tail thumped the floor. Now she knew she had been clever, and her eyes shone with pride in her splendid puppies. John took the small, cold one outside and put it down on the muck heap in the yard. He would bury it later.

Matthew Ratton came down the hill path to collect his post. It was a good, warm spring day and pleasant to walk in. Matthew's letters were left at Pennant with the Daveys to save the postman a journey, and to save Matthew the trouble of greeting him. Since the fire he had not wanted anyone's company and the Daveys, though they were his good friends and grieved for him, respected his feelings and kept out of his way, leaving his occasional letters on a shelf in the wash-house. They would be ready to talk when he felt like talking.

They had been there that day when Matthew had come staggering out of the burning ruin of the cowhouse, carrying the dead dog in his arms, its coat and his hair well on fire, and a ghastly, blackened blister down one side of his face from temple to jaw. Matthew had been rushed to hospital, and within a few days old man Ratton was dead too, of shock or heartbreak, or a bit of both. They had lost the barn and a year's supply of hay, the cowhouse and the tractor shed. No one was sure even now who had started it, but the thought was that it was probably the hot sun on broken glass left by some careless picnicker or passer by, tempted by the softness of the hay where the bales had broken to have a rest and a drink, and then to go on elsewhere, having murdered a man's livelihood without even being aware of it.

Matthew crossed the yard to the washhouse, and found two letters: one from his bank and one from the Clipton Feed Mills, telling him of the immense profits he could make if he fed his cattle on their latest concentrates. So the one would tell him he had no money, and the other would tell him to spend it. It was hardly worth the walk.

He turned for the homeward journey and as he did so he saw the pup lying on the steaming midden, and he bent down to it. So Mag had thrown one out, had she? He picked up the small thing. Should he go and see the live pups? He knew Mag well and she was a nice bitch. Used her mouth a bit too much for his liking, but a good working dog nonetheless. No, there was no point him looking. He had no need of a dog just now anyway. Since he had taken over the farm after his father's death he had sold stock left and right to pay off debts and start new buildings. Dad had never kept up with the insurance payments. The money they got after the fire would have rebuilt them twenty years ago, but not at today's prices. He thought people probably laughed at him round about, with his handful of Clun ewes with their ram, and his Ayrshires, the ones Trig had saved for him. He would have been better off out of dairying altogether he knew that. Beef and sheep went much better together. Still, he would keep the old girls for a while yet, and they did well on his lush lower pastures. He was not bothered by the endless routine of milking, either. The very regularity of it soothed him, and after all, a cow doesn't care what your face looks like.

He put a hand to his face and touched the scars. He had to touch them. Like a sharp tooth, like a splinter in the thumb, he was aware of them all the time, although the pain was long since gone, except in the hot sun when the skin grew taut, and half the time then he felt it was remembered pain, not real.

In his other hand, the tiny puppy lay limp as rag. Its face carried a white flash, triangular, like Trig's. Memory blinded his eyes for a moment.

He could feel the pulse beating in his thumb, where his hand closed round the pup's ribs. Then, mingling with that rhythm, there was suddenly another, faint and thready. He took his thumb away, and felt the ribs carefully with listening fingers. So the odd little object was not dead. Without any expressible reason for doing it, he tucked the pup inside his shirt and huddled his jacket round it. The little creature was cold and damp and smelt of muck.

Matthew strode off up the hill to his house. Flint Hill was a sizeable place, built sensibly of stone, and built for purpose rather than beauty. One end of it was buried in the rising bank, the other stood out against the prevailing wind with walls almost three feet thick. It had been standing there three centuries and there was no reason to doubt it would stand a further three at least. Behind it the sheep pastures rose up close-bitten and springy; below, it looked across its own woods and the woods of the upper valley, and the fields of Pennant Farm, pleasantly green now that the year was shifting into summer at last. The windows of the house were few and small, to keep out the westerlies that blew up the valley, and inside the house the floors were all flagstoned at ground level, and boarded in solid oak above. Matthew scarcely bothered to go upstairs these days. He lived in the kitchen and slept in the old still-room beyond. Sometimes, in winter, he did not even bother with that, but stretched out like old Lob in front of the range in the kitchen, on an old camp bed that had been his father's in the war.

Matthew walked through the yard and into the garden. It was a mass of tangled weeds and flowers: a riot of growth where once his mother's trim herbaceous borders had been. He only had time for the vegetables, and the flowers must fend for themselves. Anyway, he liked the wildness of it, and so did the bees. That gate had dropped on its hinge again, though, and must be attended to.

Once in the kitchen, Matthew looked about him for somewhere to put the pup. There was a wooden box full of tins in the corner, so he emptied it and put an old sweater in the bottom, patting it round to make a nest-shape. Then he took the pup out from under his jacket and put her into the box. She looked very tiny and lay very still, but that faint heart-beat proclaimed her alive, even if only just.

He warmed some goat's milk on the range. The fire was kept alight all year except when the chimney was due to be cleaned. Dan Ratton had always disposed of the soot by firing a shotgun up the flue, but Matthew preferred more conventional means. It was an old-fashioned hulk, the range, but it made a warm refuge in the house for weak and ailing creatures of all kinds, as well as cooking all Matthew's meals in its black hole of an oven.

Through the back window of the kitchen he could see old Bella the goat tethered on the bank. It was a good thing she was well in milk. She had had a billy-kid this year, which Matthew had knocked on the head at birth: no point in raising useless creatures. She was a fine milker, though, old Bella. He had nearly got rid of her when he was cutting down on stock, for with twelve Ayrshires he had more than enough to do, without a goat needing hand-milking twice a day, but he was glad now he had not. Flint Hill had always kept a goat, and Dan

Ratton had firmly believed that goat's milk beat any other kind for orphan creatures. To be sure, Bella and her predecessors had provided nourishment for lambs, calves and foals whose mothers could not, or would not, feed them. The Rattons had got first prize one year at Clipton Show with an Ayrshire heifer that had been raised on goat's milk. They never did tell the judge.

Matthew looked at the small, still shape of the pup and considered that she was too tiny to drink from the lamb's titty-bottle, and that he would have to think of something else. Somewhere, he remembered, there was an eye-dropper Dad had used when his eyes were sore, so he went and rummaged about upstairs until he found it. It was cold upstairs, even on such a mild day, and smelt of damp and disuse. Matthew was glad to get back to the kitchen.

He sat down in a chair by the range and scooped his strange find out of the box. One of his hands could encompass her entirely. It stirred him to think that such a tiny thing had so steadfastly refused to die. The first thing was to get the pup conscious if he could. There was no point trying to feed her till then, or she would only choke. When the lambs were born weak and cold he could often shock them into life with a teaspoonful of brandy and there was no reason that should not work with a dog. There was surely nothing to lose, because if he did not try it, that last flicker of life would snuff out and there would be nothing to do but bury her. He poured some of the fierce amber stuff into an egg-cup, dipped his finger in and pushed it gently between her jaws so that the vapour would fill her mouth and maybe stimulate the lungs. She lay on his lap on the old sweater and he rubbed her gently with his other hand.

It seemed a very long time that he went on doing this and his arm was beginning to ache, when he saw a slight movement from her tongue, and a shudder of breath expanded her ribs and her breathing grew stronger.

'Come on then,' he said to her. 'You've come this far. Don't go back on me now. Just try some of this.'

He tucked the end of the dropper into the soft fold of skin at the corner of her mouth and gently squeezed the bulb, so that one drop of milk reached her throat. With the forefinger of his other hand he rubbed her gullet to make her swallow. It was a real triumph when she did, and he felt quite ridiculously pleased.

In a quarter of an hour he had persuaded a tablespoonful of milk into her and she was no longer dying. The clammy coldness had left her, her tongue was pink, and her ribs moved in and out so that the eye could clearly watch them, instead of having to peer closely for the slight, shallow movement of before.

Matthew felt that if he could keep her really warm she would do well now. She should have a source of heat close by, as she would if she were lying in a tumble of other pups by their mother. He tucked her back inside his shirt again while he went to look for a solution to this next problem, and he could feel her tiny, soft claws against his skin. At last he found an old stone cider-jar, and filled it with hot water. Stood upright in a corner of the pup's box, and lagged with a piece of old blanket, it would make a good warm thing for her to cuddle against.

He fished her out from inside his shirt; she was asleep, but breathing well, and there were little movements under the blind lids of her eyes to show that it was nothing deeper than sleep. It would be over a week before her eyes would open and let her see the world.

She was very black. The only white on her, apart from the triangle on her face, was a white front paw, the left one, and a white tip to her tail. Otherwise she was jet black. That should be her name then, Jet. Short, simple, easy to call. That was proper for a good working dog's name. You could not bellow up a windy hill 'Come-by, Sebastian' or 'Heel, Peppermint'. Mot, Fly, Tag, Gyp, those were the names of the dogs round here. Now he had his Jet. You're a fool, he told himself. He had one spoonful of milk down her and already he had named her. It was one chance in a hundred she would survive at all.

He had to leave her then, to go out to see to his beasts. At least there was daylight now to see to the evening jobs. He remembered the time before they had electricity at Flint Hill, when all the winter chores were done by lantern light, and every cow was milked by hand. It was not so long ago: only twenty years, and even now he thought of electricity as a luxury and was sparing of it.

When he went back indoors he was almost afraid to look at the pup, but she was sleeping. Later he fed her again, drop by drop, before he sat down to his own evening meal, and afterwards, having cleared the table to do his paper work, he set the box down by his feet so that he could watch her.

That night he slept by the fire, alongside the box, getting up every couple of hours to feed her again and to refill the jar with hot water. Once, in that very early morning watch before it even begins to grow light, he sat with the pup on his knees and looked over to the empty corner where Trig had always slept.

'Well, old lass,' he said softly, 'do you think I'm daft, or what?' He still could not get out of the ten years' habit of talking to her. Trig wouldn't think he was daft, but most would. A busy man trying to scratch a living out of a small farm has got better things to do than play nursemaid to an orphan pup whose own mother felt the job wasn't worth the trouble.

There was no point in going back to sleep, so he sat and nursed Jet until light began to fringe the horizon to the east, and it was milking time again. Coming up ten thousand times his day had started like this. The other patients in the hospital had groaned at the early morning waking there, but Matthew, even on his worst days, had been awake long before the nurses came round with the tea.

He tucked Jet into her box, got ready, and went out into the fresh, cool morning. He could see the herd assembled at the gate, regarding him soberly. He walked down and opened the gate for them, and they waited for Flo, their leader, to make the first move. She ambled past Matthew on the familiar route to her stall, her udder huge, her hips swinging to accommodate its bulk.

Soon the cowhouse was full of the sweet rhythm of milking and the solemn contentment of cattle at their rations.

In the kitchen, by the fire, the pup lay warm and replete. Her nose was pressed against the heat of the cider-jar and the wooden box was filled with the tiny noise of her snoring.

CHAPTER 3

Each morning, for the next few days, it seemed to Matthew no less than miraculous to find Jet still alive when he woke. His life became punctuated by her small demands.

Soon she opened milky-blue eyes and gazed at him unseeingly, not yet focused and yet with recognition. He wondered what she perceived of him. He must seem huge to her, and yet she accepted this vast shadow as the source of food and comfort and would move towards him as he approached, her nose questioning the air, her thin little rat-like tail quivering excitedly. He had looked after puppies enough in his time, but he had never had one as young as this so entirely dependent on him.

He would feed her, and then, as she had no other company but his, and he felt that she must be lonely, he would sit with her cupped in his hands and she would sigh and make soft noises like a small happy pig, and eventually fall asleep, when he would quietly return her to her box. In everything he had to be her surrogate mother, even to sponging her with a warm cloth to act the part of the bitch's tongue, to clean her and to stimulate her bladder. She grew visibly under his care and was changing so rapidly that he felt he must record her as she was, so he took pencil and paper and drew her as she lay asleep in her box, her pink belly upturned and rounded with food. He drew every detail of her, every hair. Lightning sketches, quick impressions, were not his style: he needed to satisfy his eye, to record every minute part of her that he saw, so she appeared on the page, a small, black, collie pup complete to the last whisker, even to the remaining droplet of milk that clung to that whisker. For the first time in months, when he had finished, he did not tear out and crumple the page and hurl it into a corner, but put it away, carefully, in the drawer of the dresser.

As soon as he felt that he really could take her survival for granted, he began to carry her about with him in his pocket. It was the same jacket that had brought Trig home all those years ago, and would have been tight across the shoulders by now had the fabric not slackened with age and long wearing. The pocket sagged like a pouch and it was an ideal size for Jet to sit in and see her world, without, as yet, encountering too many of its dangers.

He took her with him on his occasional trips in the Landrover too. About the farm, Matthew much preferred to walk. You notice more, in his opinion, when you went on foot: a broken gate, a sagged fence, a lame cow or a sickly lamb; but when he had to go further afield he used the old canvas-top Landrover which had been his father's. The old man had driven it for years with supreme disregard for all the principles of mechanics, but it still went, and

Matthew saw no reason to change it. Once they drove across to the other side of the valley to look over a farm sale where he might pick up a piece or two of equipment to replace things he had lost in the fire. It was rubbishy stuff, he thought, though, not worth bidding for, and he set off for home with more of the day to spare than he had reckoned on. Then he saw a gateway that he recognized and pulled the Landrover to the side of the road. He had not been here for years, and had almost forgotten it.

He had not been one for playing truant from school, but he had done it once, on a day that was too good to miss sitting indoors. He had got off the bus unnoticed when it stopped to pick up passengers, and had set off into the blue, heedless, unplanned, letting adventure take him where it would, and he had eventually arrived at this same gateway where he now stood, and had seen a long and inviting avenue of limes stretching away to a distant and hidden house.

It was called Old Place, the ruined home of some obscure and now entirely forgotten family. It had been derelict when Matthew first found it, and the tangled trees and overgrown drive made it plain that it still was so. He had spent a whole summer's day there, all those years ago, feeling almost like a ghost himself in that pleasantly ghostly place.

Set among the blurred outlines of a once formal garden, he had come across a stone plinth, and crouched upon it the stone figure of a Great Dane, perpetually staring, eternally watchful, with ears alert and great knuckled forepaws stretched before him. He remembered that there had been an inscription underneath but he had forgotten the words.

Matthew would not drive down the avenue. He felt he must walk, as he had done before. He put Jet in his pocket and set off under the lime trees, wondering a little what he would say if he were challenged, but the whole place was as it had been before, with the additional dilapidation of years, but it was quite clear that for some reason it had never been re-inhabited. It was as if no time had passed since he was here before. The house, eyeless and forsaken, like Samson at Gaza, held no attraction for him. It was the garden he had come back to see and the great stone dog.

He found the statue, mossier and danker than he remembered it. He had to pull away brambles to read the inscription which he remembered the moment it came to light again. Carved into the stone in good formal Roman, still clearly incised in spite of time and weeds and weather, was a line of Edmund Spencer's:

'All for love and nothing for reward.'

Matthew recalled now that he had wondered what the dog had done to deserve this splendid memorial. Had he pulled some favourite child from the dark lake that lay below the house, or warned the family of impending disaster, or saved the young heir from murderous attack? It came to Matthew that his boyish romancing had imagined all these things, but now it seemed to him far more likely that the dog had won such praise just by his existence, by the devotion of his impressive and dignified self to the family that had once lived there. He took Jet out of his pocket and set her down between the massive fore-paws. She looked ridiculously comical, sitting with her head on one side, looking at him as if trying to puzzle out why she had been set on this lofty perch.

'Will you deserve a pedestal then?' he asked her. 'What will you save me from, I wonder?' and he laughed, and she let out at him her first real bark, which so surprised her that she nearly fell off the plinth.

They stayed in the garden a good hour. Consciously he took time out for them, and set aside the work waiting to be done, the worries waiting for considera-tion, and all the emotions, motives, reactions, fears that exercised his mind daily. For that short time they stayed together in the garden of his boyhood, wild and hidden, with its hot sun and tangled grass and its smell of herbage and sapply flowers.

It was soon over, though, this small retreat from reality and they had no sooner reached the gateway than the mood of the day changed. Lying in the ditch near the Landrover Matthew found a rabbit. Being a farmer, he was no friend to the rabbit. The furry little fellow in the blue coat and silver buttons was a nursery fantasy: the reality was a flea-ridden eater of crops and profits, and a despoiler of good grazing. Even so, Matthew was sickened by the sight of the animal that crouched in the ditch: huge-headed, bolt-eyed and on the point of death. There had been several outbreaks of myxomatosis in the area and although some rabbits were immune, many were to be found squatting like this one, waiting to die.

Matthew had taken rabbits by gun, by snare, by ferret and by net, and had made a good meal of his catch. He knew many a family that would have starved on poor commons without rabbit meat to go in the pot. It was a pest, the rabbit, but it gave good sport and made good eating, and now it was condemned to a foul death and made fit to feed nothing but crows. He took a short thick stick from the hedge and gave the creature a quick end.

Others were affected by the dwindling rabbit population. In the summer months the foxes thought to feed well off the warrens round Shepley, but the old white-tipped dog fox that lived in the bracken above Pennant grew tired of waiting by the unused rabbit-trails and began to develop a taste for chickens. John Davey had taken a shot at him once or twice, and warned off, the sly red fellow had turned his attention to the Flint Hill hens instead.

One night a week or so later he paced the netting and scratched at the boards of the hen-house, so much that the birds clucked and fluttered nervously, waking Matthew, who came out with his gun, but by then the fox had melted into shadow.

Jet looked at him inquiringly when he

returned, aware that something was not quite as it should be, and that clinging to her master's clothing was a harsh, rank smell that made her hair rise.

'That's fox, that is,' he told her. 'I'll set you on him, shall I?' He laughed and rolled her over and scratched her belly.

'Go to sleep, you little bitch,' he said. 'It's a while till morning.'

At first light Matthew was busy, as always, with the cows, and while he was indoors after milking, having his breakfast, the hens found a weak place in the wire where the fox had pawed it away from the staples. They made good their escape and headed for the garden. A pretty sight they were: six Rhode-Islands, glossy-feathered and sprightly, and ten Cuckoo-Marans in their demure grey dresses. The cockerel was a Maran too, and though he wore the same sober colours and did not display the usual cockerel finery of gaudy feathers, the swaggering, arrogant masculinity of his stride showed his status just as clearly. He led the way with a lordly air, his harem, in proper hierarchical order, following in train.

There they were, in the vegetable patch, when Matthew came out again, scratching in the young plants and making dust baths for themselves.

Jet had followed Matthew out of the house. She was eight weeks old now, full of life and mischief, eating everything he set before her and following him like a shadow whenever he would allow it. Now she looked carefully at the hens and considered them.

Matthew was not much of a gardener, but he liked to grow enough for his own needs: potatoes and beans, a handful or so of peas.

'Be damned to you,' he shouted at the hens. They watched him beadily and went on with their scratching. Angrily he lobbed a stone into the middle of them, but that only set them squawking and flapping for a moment before they returned to the business of dusting themselves. Then came Jet from behind Matthew, ears alert, watching the birds. The deep instinct in her drew her towards them, and as she went, she crouched, and Matthew watched her, to see what she would do.

Small though she was, the hens knew authority when they saw it, and with a mixture of luck and inbred skill she got them penned in a corner of the vegetable patch, where they quarked and clucked, but dared not come past her. Matthew was delighted. To be sure, it was instinct rather than cleverness on her part, but you could never say for sure how strong that instinct would be in any given pup, and it was not something you could teach them. With Jet, her willingness to herd things had just been declared to him and he knew he had a good dog there. Otherwise, he might as well try to teach a tone-deaf child to be a concert pianist.

Between them they returned the disgruntled, disapproving hens to their proper territory and Matthew fetched a hammer to repair the netting. Jet lay by the run and dared them to try their tricks again. Matthew praised her lavishly and made up his mind to show her the sheep before long. It felt strange to have some prospect that excited him. He had spent months living each day as it came, glad to see the back end of each as it went, its job done, its routine complete. He had been piling up stones. Now he was beginning to see what it was he might eventually build.

CHAPTER 4

The year grew and Jet flourished. She lost her milk teeth and her puppy-fluff and became a slender young dog with a shining, silky coat and an elegant, plumed tail. There was quality about her, a spare, fine quality, without daintiness. She grew strongly-muscled as a greyhound and developed a tireless energy that could carry her across any country. She took the long hill slopes in her stride.

Early on Matthew had shown her the sheep, but he had kept her in check and would not let her do more than look at them, though she quivered with eagerness. He had made her sit and watch them where they grazed with their well-grown lambs. They had raised their heads and looked at her with mild inquiry, but once they had realized she had no immediate business with them, they went back to their nibbling, uncon-cerned.

Slowly and with infinite patience, he had taught her her early lessons, the basic commands that every dog must learn who is to be more of a help than a hindrance. She had been a cleanly creature about the house right from the beginning. He had had no trouble there, and getting her to come to him was easy. He was the first creature she had recognized as another living being. He was her food-source, her comfort, her protection. It was her wish to come to him, to be with him. More difficult was teaching her to stay while he moved away from her, and although she learned early what was required of her, she would watch him be-seechingly, and sometimes if he turned his back on her and then glanced quickly round, he would catch her inching for-ward on her elbows, hoping not to be noticed. Before long though she would stay, rock-still, even if he moved out of sight, come to him on command, move away forward from him, drop down flat at a distance. All this was achieved by a combination of her natural intelligence and desire to please and Matthew's patient handling and delight in her progress.

Later in the summer, when he moved the chickens to an ark in the four-acre so that they could scratch about the grass by day and pick up some of their own provender, he took Jet with him each evening to check that they had all returned to the ark so that he could shut them in safe against foxes, who were still looking for an easy food-source for their gawky, half-grown cubs. Jet's job was to persuade indoors any hen who was reluctant to go to bed.

She made mistakes, sometimes, like any young creature, but Matthew seldom raised his voice to her. She knew well enough his tone when he was displeased, and she learned quickly.

When he was really satisfied that she was ready for it, he put a couple of old ewes in a circular pen made of sheepwire and stakes and let her run round outside to make her circle them, and to teach her to keep her distance. He was glad that, unlike Mag, she was not a noisy dog and was rarely tempted to bark. Using the pen, he was able to teach her to circle away from him, to the left or to the right, on the command 'Come by' or 'Away to me', and then he taught her the whistled signals for the same commands, so that to voice or to whistle she would move to right or left, run or creep forward or lie down flat, and still as a stone. Words he used when she was close at hand, but the whistled commands would reach her even when she was working at furthest distance.

Still, sometimes, he would speak to Trig, as though she were there, watching them.

'How was that then, Trig? OK is she?' Or as if consulting her, 'D'you think she's ready to work them closer now?'

He had thought once that he would never work as well with a dog again, after Trig. There had been dogs at the farm before and they had died, and he had been sad at the ending of a good working partnership, and then the feeling had passed. Trig had been different. He had never been able to admit to anyone, in that practical community, how much he had grieved for her, and he had shocked himself by the realization that he ached more for the loss of her than for the loss of his father.

Now he had Jet, and he felt that Trig approved of her. He would never forget Trig, but it was as if she had lain herself down quietly in a corner of his mind and that would be her measure of immortality. Jet was full of life, demanding, keen. He was careful to make her take things steady. He thought of the bad old times when a keen dog would have a forepaw thrust through a rope collar, or even deliberately maimed, to slow it down in its work. Jet learned to curb herself at once at the sound of his voice. He loved to see her crouch to her work in an intensity of concentration, ears cocked back to his voice or whistle. He thought how some dogs obeyed only because they were afraid to disobey, and was glad of Jet's eager spirit. She looked happy in her work, too, never cowed. A collie's method of working, crouching, running close to the ground with head down, sometimes gives the impression of a creature over-dominated, almost afraid: sometimes with justification. Jet had no cause to be afraid of Matthew, though he allowed himself no sentiment where she was concerned. Still, wherever he was, she was, and she slept warm in the kitchen, and when he ate, so did she.

By the year's end she could lift and gather and drive the sheep skilfully and quietly, and the sheep took to her. They respected her and Matthew supposed that right in the back of their woolly brains there was an element of fear of her too, but she did not make them nervous. Matthew had known sheepdogs, well-trained and well-bred, who nevertheless communicated this disruptive, jumpy feeling to the flock and were well-nigh useless as a result.

So Matthew and Jet worked the sheep

and drove the cattle together day after day, and as time went by Matthew began to find himself properly attentive again for things needing to be done. For so long he had been unable to care at all, and had done the necessary jobs simply because they were there to be done and it would not have occurred to him to neglect them. But there had been no enthusiasm.

It was a day in late May: the first real taste of good weather. Matthew was in the near meadow looking appraisingly at the flock. He could increase the numbers now he had Jet to work them. He would keep most of the ewe-lambs on, maybe. He looked up the hillside to the rough sheepwalks above Tally Cottage and wondered whether he might not see about renting them when Tom Fielding's lease ran out. It had been in Dan Ratton's mind to put in for them when the time came. The flock that grazed there went with the tenancy, and they were a roughish lot, but Matthew could improve them over the years with his own good blood, and cull the worst of them. He grinned lopsidedly at his own eagerness. He compared himself now with what he had been like the previous May. He had come a long way, he felt, in himself. He still had little use for other people, but he had made himself useful enough, and Flint Hill was beginning to show it.

'It's all your fault, little bitch,' he said to Jet, as they sat in the lee of a wall, watching the new season's lambs playing their leaping games on the trunks of some felled trees. She put her chin on his knee and looked up at him under her brows. It was almost exactly a year since he had found Jet on the muck-heap, and so occupied had he been with her raising and her training that it had slipped by with amazing swiftness, the more amazing after the long, slow, dragging months that had followed the fire. In all that year the nightmare had come to him less and less, and now his dreams were scarcely troubled.

'It's all your fault, see?' he said to her

again. 'Come on now, there's work to be done.'

* * * *

John Davey leaned out of the cab of the truck and waved goodbye to his wife. He was going to pick up Matthew's wether lambs for the Clipton market. It had not been a bad season, all things considered, and with luck they would fetch a fair price.

Well, if he drove up slowly Matthew should have time to get them down to the yard ready for him. He had seen, from the Pennant gate, Matthew and Jet set out up the track to where the lambs grazed. What a marvel that dog was. So often a dog raised by hand never came to much, and seldom had the whipcord quality of a working dog. OK for a pet maybe, but not much else. Well, Jet had proved the exception. John remembered how astonished he had been when Matthew had first told him about the pup. He had walked up to Flint Hill one day, determined to make Matthew the offer of the best of Mag's litter, thinking it was high time Matthew had another dog, but half afraid of the reception he would get for suggesting it. He had been chary of passing more than a few words with him ever since the terrible day of Dan Ratton's funeral, which Matthew had insisted on attending, though heavily bandaged and hardly able to stand.

It ought always to rain at funerals, but at old man Ratton's the sun had shone in heartless glory, hot as the day of the fire, and in a field beyond the graveyard a tractor had clanked and rattled, almost drowning the rector's voice, as it turned on the headland. Once, when Shepley was a smaller place, the whole village would have stood still for the funeral, with quietness and drawn blinds, but time was money now.

With the picture in his mind of Matthew Ratton standing determinedly upright at the graveside, as unaware of people round him as if he were a granite cliff, John Davey had gone cautiously to the door of Flint Hill and knocked. That was nearly a year ago, but the scene was clear in John Davey's memory. Matthew had come to the door with Jet tucked under his arm—she had still been a tiny thing then—and he had pushed the pup under John's nose and said, half jesting, half fierce, 'Come to get your dog back, have you?'

Slowly, since that day, some of the past easiness between the older man and the younger had returned. Matthew no longer fended off all John Davey's friendliness as if on a stone wall, though he still preferred his own company and Jet's to anyone else's. He was glad enough, though, when John had offered to take the Flint Hill wether lambs to market with his own, for Matthew's flock being so small now, there was only a dozen to go, and he was glad to save on time and transport.

That morning, as John Davey had seen, Matthew took Jet with him to bring them down to the yard. She was well-grown now, sleek and glossy as a blackbird.

The lambs were in the Wally Field. It was a good field, with a sound bottom of springy turf that brought the lambs on well without being too rich. It was called Wally because a high stone wall had once run the whole length of it, but the wall was tumbled in places and patched with sheep-wire. Matthew would get round to rebuilding it, some day. He knew how to build wall. His father had taught him. Miss Atherly had been right: the old man had skills worth the learning. A good wall, well-built, kept sheep in better than anything, and would last a hundred years or more if it were built sound in the first place. This one had been here longer than anyone could remember. He picked up some fallen stones and stacked them, enjoying fitting each against each so that they stayed secure. Yes, he would build up the wall again, in the back-end of the year when there was more time.

He felt Jet press eagerly against him. The lambs were nibbling, but watchful, beginning to bunch together instinctively.

One began to move a little faster and then leapt an imaginary obstacle in its path. One after the other of its companions did the same. They were full of themselves, bounding stiff-legged like spring-heeled Jacks in the warmth of the sun. They would not be easy to work. Jet was eager to gather them up, but he made her wait, deliberately. She must go at the word and not before. She quivered all over, waiting for his voice, her eyes on the sheep.

He spoke and she was gone, moving right-handed round them. They bunched obediently, except for one who turned and stepped towards her. She dropped flat and eyed the lamb much as a nanny might stare at a small child mis-behaving at a party. The lamb retreated as if abashed and joined its fellows. She let them settle, then brought them on, straight and steady, to where Matthew stood with the gate held open for her.

'Good lass,' he said.

The little flock flowed through the gateway and out on to the turfy track that led down to the yard. Then suddenly a horse, the hoofbeats muffled to silence by the soft grass, came cantering round the angle of the wall and the lambs scattered.

'Damn,' said Matthew. He liked horses, but he did not much care for the sort of people that owned them these days. He sent Jet to gather the flock again and glared at the rider. It was a girl, sitting there so high on the big bay horse. His eyes did not register her face at all. She had her back to the sun and the brightness dazzled him, but he saw that she was a slender girl, almost spare. No one local, that was for sure. Posh young lass by the look of her, and all done up like a dog's dinner—jodhpurs and boots and well-cut jacket, her hands gloved, her hair caught back in a knot below her riding hat; not a bit like the scruffy kids that came galloping about his land from time to time. He would have taught them to know better than to scatter his flock. Oddly, he felt irritated by her neatness, the calm look of her, and the ease with which she sat the animal she rode, as much as by the result of her action.

'Should have more sense,' he muttered, and turned away, looking to see that Jet had all the lambs under her eye again.

'I'm very sorry,' the girl said. 'I just didn't see the sheep until it was too late.'

'You can say that again,' Matthew said crossly. He kept his face turned from her, as if still occupied with the dog. 'What were you doing here anyway?'

She walked the horse forward a few paces.

'It's a bridlepath, isn't it? If I was trespassing, then I'm sorry, I didn't know.'

'Aye, it's a bridlepath,' he said, as if he could well do without its being any such thing. 'Not many use it these days.'

He began to walk on with Jet. As far as he was concerned there was no need to speak further, but she called after him.

'Would you rather I didn't use it?'

'Can't stop you,' he shouted back, his voice surly. 'Come on, Jet.'

As the track curved round towards the farm he saw the horse cantering on up the hill, moving elegant as a dancer. A thoroughbred, most likely, Matthew thought, and worth more than he could make in a year.

He and Jet penned the lambs in the yard and soon, in the distance, he could hear John Davey's cattle-truck wheezing up the track to fetch them. Matthew sat down on the lip of the water-trough to wait for it. The grey stone of the buildings round him soaked up the warm sun. Beyond the yard wall the grass was growing well now: lush and green on the lower meadows, and springy and close on the hillside. Every year it was the same, the sudden upsurge of green from the drabness of winter; yet always, in a cold and lingering January, or a suddenly freezing March, there lurked in Matthew a suppressed and primitive fear, only half-admitted even to himself, that this year it might not be so. He supposed that all men who worked the land must feel it at some time. Civilization is a thin enough varnish anyway, but out among the hills it could scrape away at a touch and let you see reality.

Matthew looked round at all the land that was his, from the Pennant boundary wall to the green arc where the hill met the sky. It blended softly from green to blue today. When it stood out sharp and clear, then it would be stormy before dark. This was the place then whose more or less unwilling servant he had been since his brother's death. The fire that had made Matthew master of it at such cost had at the same moment almost lost it for him entirely, with outbuidings ruined, stock depleted and funds stripped out so that the bank clamoured for money that did not exist. And in the threat of losing it, through some odd contrariness of the mind, by some alchemy whose process he had been unaware of, he had come to realize that he loved the place. It was his and he would starve to death in it rather than give it up. He was surprised at the ferocity of his own feelings. After all, the house was mostly empty, with just himself and the dog in it, there was more to be done on the farm than he would ever get round to, and it would take a miracle to pay off all he owed. He was a fool, he supposed. Still, he stretched his legs out on the warm cobbles and felt satisfied.

CHAPTER 5

The more Matthew worked with Jet, the closer he felt to her, and the more he realized what a worthy successor she was to his beloved Trig. Jet was eager, obedient, intelligent, and her few mistakes were never repeated. Sometimes he could swear she could read his mind. Like Trig, she was patient with the cows and never hurried them, though she stood no nonsense from Sal, who was the cranky one and quite capable of raking her with her huge horns. The younger cows were polled, but Sal was elderly and crowned with wicked spiked handlebars that could do a deal of mischief if they caught you. Fortunately she was kindly disposed to her companions in the herd as long as they remembered their place, but with people she was never predictable, and though Matthew would not consider parting with her because of her prodigious milk yield, he was always wary of her. Only that morning as she passed him in the milking shed she had swung her head and lunged at him, but Jet had been there, quick as light, giving her nose a sharp nip and sending her off to her stall, cross and frustrated.

Well, Jet would be busy today. It was time to dip the sheep. It was the second dipping of the year for Matthew's flock. He dipped them in late spring to stop them getting fly-struck, and now, in September, it was time again. At dipping and shearing a good dog was worth three or four extra men. Matthew thought of the days when Flint Hill numbered its sheep in hundreds and the dogs would work tirelessly all day. He was a small boy then and looked forward to the excitement of it, with the contract men coming in for the shearing and the table always loaded with enormous meals for them. There was one old man he could just remember who sheared with the old hand-clippers and could leave a sheep looking like a clinker-built boat, the neat, overlapping ridges deliberately left to help shed the rain from the new-shorn beast until its wool grew long enough for protection again. He could not do that with the electric clippers, nor be as neat, though he was a shade faster, no doubt.

Now Matthew could shear all he had alone and the only company apart from Jet's that he had at the dipping was Jack Walsh, known as the Agriculture Man, who came to make sure the September dipping was done according to regulations, to keep the sheep scab at bay as well as to kill off the fly that laid its eggs beneath the fleece, and the keds and ticks that could make a sheep's life a misery and rob it of condition. No good shepherd would fail to dip his sheep and Matthew would have resented Jack's coming if Jack had not been careful to make a joke of it himself. Round here, if you said you had dipped your sheep, your word should be good enough, but it was not good enough, it seemed, for the men who sat in offices in the town, sending out reminders and approvals and application forms and licences, and had probably never got mud on their boots, if boots they ever wore. One year, Matthew remembered, Jack Walsh had been ill, and they had sent out some dapper little fellow in a good suit and shiny shoes. Dan Ratton had stumped off in disgust, muttering that he wouldn't be taught to suck eggs by *that*, and Matthew, left to cope on his own, had contrived to get the little man thoroughly soaked in sheep-dip by the time he left.

Well, at least today was about right for the job; not too hot, but with no wind to chill the wet sheep as they stood about. The best of September weather, in fact. They had been penned since early in the day, and the dip-bath was ready. Jack Walsh's van was bumping along the track to the yard.

'You ready then, Jet?' Matthew asked. She waved her tail at him and took up her position by the sheep-pen gate. Matthew had not seen Jack Walsh since the fire, for his flock had been so small the previous year that John Davey had taken the sheep down to Pennant and dipped them with his own. Now, for a moment, Matthew felt the old desire to hide, to avoid facing the initial reaction of yet another person who had last seen him as he used to be and now had to see him as he was. But all Jack Walsh said was, 'New cowhouse looks good.'

Matthew had spent most of the insurance money on it, so it needed to be. The rest he would repair himself, as he could find time and funds, and had already accomplished a good deal, but to watch the cowhouse go up had been even in the days of his worst desolation, some kind of comfort to him. Cows must be milked and there must be a fit place to do it, no matter what things might lurk in the shadows of the mind.

'It'll do,' Matthew said.

'Well, I've come to show you how to do your job again. We'll get on with it, shall we?'

'Right,' said Matthew.

Jack Walsh was not one to stand in a

corner and watch another man work. He lent a welcome hand with the sheep and soon the animals were plunging into the pungent dip, to be thrust unwillingly under the surface for a moment or so, after which they emerged spluttering and outraged like elderly maiden aunts who have suffered a ducking.

The sun came out and the day grew hotter. It was as well they had made an early start. Soon all the dipped sheep stood round them, dripping wetly and stinking of disinfectant and the two men straightened their backs to take a breather. Then Matthew heard hoofbeats and turned to see the girl on the bay horse approaching. She called a greeting and would have waved, but the bay snorted nervously at the smell of the dip and shied away so that she needed both her hands to control him. Matthew turned his back, deliberately showing himself a busy man: far too occupied to pass the time of day with those leisured enough to be out riding on a fine horse on the hillside. Besides, she had caused enough trouble last time she came by his sheep. He'd not encourage her to ride this way.

'I see Mary West is arrived then,' Jack Walsh said. 'Come to stay with her uncle in the village, it seems. Peter West, you know, that architect fellow. You know him, don't you?'

'My dad knew his dad, I think,' Matthew said. 'Used to be farmers round here somewhere, once. Too grand for it now, I suppose.'

'She's come into some property I hear.'

'Oh...' said Matthew, and turned the conversation once again to the subject of sheep and to the prowess of Jet, who lay in the corner of the yard sunning herself and enjoying a brief rest from duty. He told Jack the story of how he had come by her and the hopes he had of building up the flock now he had a good dog to work them.

'She's a fine worker judging by today,' Jack said. 'You should take her to the trials, show her off a bit.'

'Hell as like,' said Matthew. 'She's here to work, not to show off to amuse people. Anyway, I've no time for that.'

The two men had opened bottles of beer that Matthew had brought from the house and were washing away the taste of dip and sheep-grease. Jack tipped his bottle right back to catch the last dregs, then wiped his mouth on the back of his arm.

'That was good,' he said. 'Well, you give it a thought, anyway, mister. She's good enough to win, in my opinion.'

'Maybe,' Matthew said. He knew very well she was, if he worked hard with her. He was not so sure of himself, though. It would mean facing the crowds, joining in the sheep-talk with shepherds of vast flocks, of prize-winning commercial flocks, watching him and his dog with critical, appraising eyes. She would be all right, his Jet, but his skin crawled at the idea of opening himself to it.

Peggy Davey lay awake in the big bed at Pennant Farm, with the black hulk of

John Davey asleep, lying between her and the moonlight like a cast-up ship.

As they got older she seemed to sleep less and he all the sounder. She was used to it now and did not let it worry her, but lay quietly and looked at the pattern of cracks on the ceiling and thought. Often she thought about Matthew, whom she had known and loved since he was a baby, and the nearest thing—deep in her own mind, and no one's affair but her own—to being the child she had never been able to have herself. She had been sad to be childless, but she had accepted it and would have managed quite well without, if Matthew had not happened to be there; but he had been there, and she loved him. Hannah Black had been her good friend and there was far more of Hannah than Dan in Matthew Ratton, and just as well too. Peggy could not think to this day why such a gentle, intelligent creature should have married such a man, but then there's no logic in love, and he was a handsome enough fellow when he was young. Not like her

John, with his face like a rock-fall. Listen to him snore now, loud as the old saddleback boar in the sty. She shoved him affectionately, and he rolled over, snorted, and began to breathe more quietly.

Her thoughts returned to Matthew. She had hardly set eyes on him a dozen times since the fire because she could see that it hurt him to be seen. Some people said it was self-pity, but it was more than that, less shallow than that.

When she was a girl, at the fanciful age, she had wanted to be a healer. Her mother had told her stories of a man she had met once who could put his hands on people and cure them. He would put his fingers on the place, and pray, and the pain would go. He had cured a woman of toothache and she had been so relieved she had danced about in the street.

Peggy had longed to feel the glowing warmth of a miracle at her fingers' ends. What if she could put her hands now on Matthew Ratton's face and watch the skin grow pink and clear again? Still so fanciful, after all these years. She tried to laugh at herself, but her eyes felt hot with tears that she would not acknowledge.

John Davey stirred in his sleep, turned towards her and opened his eyes.

'Still awake?' he said. 'Was I snoring?'

'Loud enough to wake yourself,' she said.

'Keep you awake, did I?'

'It wasn't you. I was just thinking.'

'Oh?'

'I met that girl of West's today. Nice girl she seems. Asked me if Matthew was always rude to people, or was it just her.'

'Oh, she's met him, has she?'

'Two or three times, apparently. She rides her horse up over that way.'

'D'you think she fancies him?'

'Don't you be coarse, John Davey.'

'I'm not being coarse, my little old love. It's a rare fine thing for a man to have a pretty girl take a fancy to him, and who should know that better than me, eh?'

'Oh, get on with you, John. I wish he'd speak to her. He's been too long by himself. It would be good for him.'

'That's as may be, my love, but he doesn't want what's good for him. He wants to be left in peace. Go to sleep now. It'll be morning soon.'

In moments he was fast asleep once more, leaving Peggy to go over in her mind again her meeting with a young girl who seemed far more concerned about Matthew's lack of courtesy than the fact that he had only half a face.

The summer was moving into autumn, each day adding to the pattern of the year, each day bringing its own small changes that only the unhurried eye would see: the flowering and fading of successive plants in field and garden, and the swelling and harvesting of fruits in their season. Matthew measured his life far more by these small events than by any calendar: the days his garden had given him great platefuls of young peas to eat; the afternoon Peggy Davey had brought him a basket of strawberries; the weeks he had spent taking hay from the bottom meadows and storing it in the barn.

Whatever he was doing, Jet was there beside him. She lay between rows in the garden when he worked there, or rode behind him on the tractor, precariously balancing her weight on its jolting motion. She followed him to Pennant to fetch the post, and John Davey would laugh and scratch her ears and say, 'How's the throw-out, then?'

On one particular evening when Matthew was crossing the Pennant yard, John Davey called out to him, 'Got some time to spare?'

'I suppose,' said Matthew.

'Well, then, will you come and celebrate an old man's birthday? I'm off to the Dog and Partridge to get myself a pint. Peg won't come: you know what she's like about women in pubs. Silly old fool she is, but she's not likely to change now, and I don't fancy drinking alone tonight. Anyway, I've told Jimmy Peel many a time what a good bitch you had out of my Magpie and he'd like to see her.'

Matthew was all for refusing. If he drank at all these days, he drank at home in the kitchen, or out in the yard or the fields when the work was thirsty and warranted a bottle or so of beer. Still, John was an old friend and he wouldn't offend him. There was hardly ever more than a handful of locals in the Dog and Partridge on a weekday evening anyway.

'All right then,' Matthew said. 'I'll stand you a pint.'

They walked on down to the village together with Mag and Jet trotting behind. The two bitches were wary of each other, their brief relationship entirely unremembered, each devoted only to the master who walked ahead of her.

In the field next to the pub, the bay horse grazed in hock-high grass, his coat gleaming gold in the low sunlight. He lifted his head as the men approached, as if he were half-expecting someone to come for him.

'That's that girl West's horse, isn't it?' John said. 'A fine beast it is. Peggy tells me you met the girl.'

'Didn't meet her. Saw her a couple of times, though. Just riding by. Upset the sheep.'

'Well she'll not upset them for a while. I hear she's gone up to London and then she's off abroad.'

'I'm not surprised,' Matthew said. 'She looked the type.' The type to be off to London for the doing of her hair and buying clothes and whatever else young women with more pounds than sense spent their time and money on, before jumping on a plane to follow the sun. Well, it would keep her off his land, anyway.

Jimmy Peel, the publican, came to the door of the Dog and Partridge and called a welcome to the two men as they approached. There had not been much custom yet. Light evenings stretched the day's work for the farming community that made up the pub's custom, and strangers, though tolerated, were not encouraged. There were pubs enough tarted up for the tourist trade with fake brasses and little bits of food in baskets.

' 'Evening John, 'evening Matthew,' Jimmy said. 'I see John's conned you into buying him a pint on his birthday.'

'You're right there,' John said. 'What else would I ask him for?'

They went into the cool bar parlour which was just a low, flagged room with benches round it and a big high bar at one end. Jimmy set their beers in front of them and put a bowl of ale-slops at Jet's nose.

'I hear she's a right good bitch,' he said, 'and a good bitch needs a drop of something now and again.'

'I'll tell my Peggy that,' said John, with a great wink and a bellow of laughter that made Jet look up in surprise.

'Go on then, lass. It's for you,' said Matthew, and she lapped the queer-tasting stuff and found she liked it.

The men talked in their corner till the light faded, and several more beers had been set before them, and John's health well and truly drunk. Matthew began to be aware that more people had drifted into the pub, enough to make quite a crowd, and for the first time in well gone a year there was no panic beating inside him. He reached down for Jet and grasped her ruff in his fingers.

'You're a good bitch,' he said, and she dusted the flag-stones with her tail in reply.

CHAPTER 6

It was October. As far as Matthew could be sure, all his cows and the two heifers were in calf, by courtesy of the AI man with his white coat and his little Mini-van. The Bull-pen at Flint Hill had been empty a good many years: the last bull had been sold when Trig was in her prime, and the few cows he had now would not justify the expense of keeping one. He used the heavily barred enclosure for penning small numbers of sheep from time to time, but he could remember its proper inmates, huge figures from his childhood memory, like Solomon, a vast red creature who had seemed to him a mountain of flesh and muscle, or Trumpeter, the first of the Ayrshire bulls, of a morose and surly temperament that had made all the men afraid of him. Yet it was Tarquin, the gentle, trustworthy fellow whose ears Matthew had scratched many times, sitting on the bars of the pen while the bull munched his hay, who had turned and knelt on the stockman one day and deliberately set about trying to kill him.

That was all in the past now. He supposed it would be more sensible to borrow a ram for his handful of ewes, too, rather than keep his own. Still, it was another fleece to sell, and anyway, his Clun ram was a beauty, a fine beast, who had never failed yet to get a ewe in lamb. He was running with the ewes now, snatching mouthfulls of grass while keeping a dominating eye on them. He looked fit and well from the high feeding Matthew had given him in the past weeks, and the ewes made it obvious they thought him no end of a fellow. They were looking good, as well, Matthew thought: nice, even, well-grown fleeces; neat, clean feet; bright, alert eyes. He was pleased with them.

He walked down to the yard, Jet as always trotting at heel, and looked round at the buildings. The new Dutch barn was stacked high with hay. The timber one that the fire had taken had been God knows how old, a solid, handsome building. Still, this one was not unpleasant to the eye, and the red-ochre paint on the iron roof would soon be matched by the leaves of the great trees behind it, when the year began to turn. The new cowhouse still looked brash and glaring though against the mellowness of the old stone, but there was no point being old-fashioned for the sake of it: he had modernized while he had the chance, and it made the milking easier. He smiled to himself, remembering the old girls' puzzled faces when they had first ambled into the new milking parlour. They were used to it now, though, and each found her proper stall, as before.

He was still rebuilding the tractor sheds, slowly, as time and money allowed, and with his own labour as he could afford no other and was not of a mind to accept charitable help. He must get the roof completed before winter came on. He climbed up to check again on the amount of timber he would need. No point in buying too much with prices as they were.

He stood for a moment, perched on top of the ladder, breathing the smell of the new joists he had lately put in and wondering to himself if the swallows would return to nest in the new roof, as they had done in the old. He had watched them swooping disconsolately round the walls in early summer, wheeling and crying out as if distressed by this alteration in the pattern of their lives. One or two had made do with the rafters in the stables, but there had been nothing like the number of mud and straw cradles that there usually were at Flint Hill, to be filled with wide-mouthed infants peevishly calling for food.

Someone was walking beneath him, and John Davey's voice called, 'That you up there, Matthew?'

Matthew squinted down at him and said, 'Who else would it be? Bloody funny place for burglars, if it's not.'

'Still not finished that roof, then?'

'No. I need more timber.'

'Well, that's what I came up about. You know Fishers' in Clipton?'

'Timber merchants, you mean? Yes, I know 'em.'

'Well, it seems they're being closed down, or bought up, or took over or what have you, and they're selling off some lots of timber at half price: joists, two-by-fours, battens and so on, and you can get off-cuts for almost nothing. Thought you might like to know.'

'Aye, thanks, John. I'll go in and have a look. Wait on a moment, I'll soon be down.'

'Don't bother, lad, Jet'll see me out. You've not got fed up with her yet, I see?'

'Not likely.' Matthew laughed, and it seemed to John Davey the most welcome sound he had heard in a good while. He rubbed Jet behind the ears, and patted her chest.

'Keep it up, girl,' he said.

Matthew took the Landrover into

Clipton that afternoon. It rattled and lurched down the stony track that joined the lane, and then they were on the minor road which weaved through the village and on to the T-junction with the main road to Clipton.

Shepley seemed deserted as he drove through. More of the women went out to work these days. More and more houses stood empty all day. The school was closed now, too, and even the smallest children were whisked away each day to school in Clipton, leaving the village as quiet as if the Pied Piper had come through with his music. Miss Atherly was long since dead and the school-house was a weekend cottage now. Still, Shepley had not declined as far as some. Most of the houses still belonged to village families, but if ever they came up for sale, you could be sure it would only be an outsider that could afford them. It was a small and straggling village, with no obvious centre, no focal point, except for the Dog and Partridge which was its only social meeting place now the school was gone, and what had once been a village store was now just a post office which stocked only the most basic goods: ancient postcards and tins of processed peas as supplied to Noah. The Dog and Partridge stood at the top end of the village, and from there the cottages ranged themselves along the village street to where Vale House and All Saints' Church stood opposite each other across the stream. There was no squire's house in Shepley, no great estate nearby to tie all the village cottages to its apron strings. Vale House, which had once been a mill, was the largest, and even that had no pretensions to splendour. The Rectory, tucked in by the side of the church, was modest, as rectories go.

It was a quiet village then, unassuming, pleasing to the eye, yet seldom attracting the tourist to make the necessary detour from the Clipton-Faverton road to visit. The guide-books for the most part did not bother to mention it at all.

There was not too much traffic on the

roads, which was a relief to Matthew, for the Landrover's engine was making bronchial noises and there was a rattling sound from somewhere that he could not trace. He would get more petrol in Clipton and give the old camel a kick. That should fix her.

Clipton was a small town, hardly grown out of being a village itself, though its High Street had recently blossomed out into neon lighting and plastic facades to match every other in the country. Still, it kept many of its old streets: grey, uncompromisingly workaday streets, but beautiful because they were old and homogenous and had been built for a purpose. It kept its central cattle-market too. This had not yet, as had so many others, been pushed to the perimeter for the sake of tidiness and the avoidance of traffic congestion. You could still be held up, on a Wednesday morning, by the contrariness of a flock of sheep, or you could have your polished bodywork shat on by an overexcited bullock as it was urged to pass, encouraged by a large stick in the hands of some small boy, off school by reason of a politic cold, in order to act as unpaid drover for the day. Matthew had done the job himself when he was small and Miss Atherly had know quite well where he was, he was sure of that. She had been far too wise to comment, though, and it had taught him to reckon figures quickly as he followed the auctioneers' rapid patter and worked out what profit, if any, the farm had made on the beasts being sold, for Dan Ratton would want to know, and there would be sore ears if Matthew could not tell him.

There was no market today though and the town was quiet. Matthew turned off through side-streets to the timberyard. He knew his way, but if he had not, he would have needed no other guide than the rasping shriek of the rip-saw and the resinous smell of fresh sawdust.

High, solid gates were painted with the sign 'Fisher and Sons, Timber Merchants' and these were opened for him by a man carrying planks on his shoulder. He drove in. There were baulks of timber and piles of sawn wood everywhere and the noise was terrific, as several circular saws, further off, were at work as well as the rip-saw. Poor Jet drooped miserably as the noise hurt her ears, and the man at the main saw-bench looked up, saw Matthew coming and pulled a switch to stop the machinery. The shrieking sound died into comparative silence, and the man called out a greeting.

'I'm Sam Hallett, foreman. Can I help you?'

'Yes,' said Matthew and stepped towards the bench. As he did so he heard the snarling of a dog. In the corner of the yard, near the office, a great grey Alsation was chained to a post and stood with raised hackles, staring and snarling, warning off Jet and her master. The yard foreman picked up a piece of sawn-off plank from under the bench and hurled it at the dog.

'Shup up your row, you bugger,' he said, and the dog slunk to the far limit of its chain and lay down.

'Gives me the willies, that dog,' the man admitted. 'He'll have one of us one of these days and that's for sure. Now, what was it you wanted?'

Matthew explained what he needed and produced a list from his pocket.

'Yes, we can do all this for you,' the foreman said, 'and you'll not be disappointed at the price. Come over to the office and I'll get a couple of lads to load up for you.'

They walked to the office door and the grey dog glared at them balefully.

'Boss used to let him run loose at night,' Sam Hallett said, 'before they put a law against it. Still, he's devil enough to frighten anyone off, chained or loose, to my way of thinking.'

'Yes,' Matthew said. 'It's as well he's not loose, not without a handler, anyway.'

'And who's to handle him, tell me that? The only thing I'd handle him with is a bullet.' Hallett laughed and showed Matthew into the office, whence two lads were dispatched to load up the Land-rover.

Matthew sat and waited, watching the comings and goings in the timber yard while his bill was reckoned up. The big gates opened again to admit a lorry and, as if to illustrate the foreman's assessment of his character, the gaunt grey dog lunged barking and growling to the end of his chain, and brought up short, choking against the collar, he glowered at the world with such hatred as Matthew had never before seen in a dog. Matthew felt sorry for the poor creature, savage though it so obviously was. He glanced down at Jet and thought what a world of difference lay between her devoted service and the grey dog's unwilling and resentful slavery. Yet she might well have been just like him, given the same treatment, for after all, he was a shepherd breed too, from the days when it was protection rather than subtle control that was needed. Here was a dog who, under different circumstances, could have been as devoted to a flock as Jet was, and yet look what had been made of him: a canine terrorist, trained to frighten and to hurt, in defence of people he would savage with equal relish if he could, and so good at the job now that no one dare trust him.

When the Landrover was ready, Matthew and Sam Hallett went out to inspect the load. Hallett made sure it was tied securely, and then said, 'You'll need a red cloth on the end of that lot: it sticks out a fair way. You don't want some fool driving himself onto it. They drive so close, some of 'em, you'd think there was naked women in your back window.'

'They'd be lucky,' said Matthew. 'This little bitch is the only female that rides in my vehicle.'

The foreman looked at Jet. 'Nice dog, that,' he commented. 'Much more style than that brute out there.'

'What'll happen to him when the yard closes down?' Matthew asked.

'God knows,' said the foreman. 'With luck, somebody'll shoot him.'

They drove home the long way round,

through Brierley and Cheriton, so as to pick up some vaccine from George Aiken, the vet. They had not gone far out of Cheriton when Matthew noticed the petrol gauge dropping ominiously near to 'empty'. He had forgotten to fill up in town. He stopped the Landrover and got out the spare can. There was enough to get him home at any rate, and John Davey would lend him some to be going on with. He would be better off with a diesel really, he supposed, and he didn't much like the noise of the old car's engine. Sounded like mice had got in somewhere.

'All in good time, though, eh Jet?' he said. 'Come on, we'll stretch our legs a while, shall we?'

They walked away across the rough grazings. These were the walks Tom Fielding rented, that ran on down to march with his own sheep pastures. There were sheep here, grazing in small bunches, whose ancestors had grazed the same hill for generations. Once Tally Cottage had been the home of the shepherds that tended them, but Tom Fielding preferred his own house in the village, and since he had come into a little money from his father he had taken small interest in the sheep, though he was determined to see his lease out, as he had paid for it.

Matthew glanced across at the sheep. They were a rough lot, but they must be hardy enough, goodness knows, to have survived the poor shepherding they had had. If he took them on, he could soon build them up again, and they would then have no need to come leaping his boundary wall as they often did in winter, stealing hay he had put out for his own flock. Trouble was, he was not sure who to approach about the lease. Fielding's rent was paid into some Trust Fund in London that acted for the owner, and Matthew distrusted organizations. He would find out who the owner was and approach him. No need approaching Fielding. He was not the friendliest of men, and close as a clam when it came to anything to do with his livelihood.

Matthew gazed downhill to where his own land began and saw with pleasure how the tussocky grass, bracken and gorse gave way to his own well-tended pastures. Dan Ratton had certainly known how to manage grassland and had taught his sons the care of every precious blade of what he called 'God's own crop'. After all, it was natural food for all the grazing creatures and none could be healthy without it. Even in the far-off days of the great work-horses, that were kept stabled for the most part and fed on good hay and corn to give them strength for their heavy labour, come Sunday they were turned out in the meadows to roll and graze. Albert, one of Dan Ratton's men, who had been a very old chap when Matthew was tiny and had been nursemaid to horses for more years than could be remembered, used to call these Sunday outings. 'Visiting Dr Green'.

Well, the grass grew of its own sweet will, but Matthew had in his bones the knowledge of when and how to graze it and when to let it rest; when to harrow it half to death and when to leave it alone; when to nibble it hard down with sheep and when to turn cattle out on it. Some of the hill-pastures never really grew long enough for the cows to wrap their tongues around, but they made ideal sweet grazing for the young lambs. Some of the lower meadows were too rich and damp ever to be grazed long by sheep, or there would be foot troubles, or hoven, which was worse, when the young stock would blow up like so many bags of gas and would have to be stuck with a trocar and cannula to save their lives. Then the gas would rush out of them and they would be on their feet again. Magic, it was.

These were the meadows that made good hay though, for the winter supplies, so each parcel of land had its own good use, and that was the hoped-for balance of the farm: each provision set against each need. Mind you, in every year something would happen to upset it to a minor extent, as is the way of things, but it was seldom anything as disastrous as the fire. Always the ideal of balance was there, indestructible. It was the only sane thing in the world, Matthew often thought.

Below and to the left of where he stood, Tally Cottage was just visible among the trees. It was a queer, tumble-down little house with one great chimney at the west end of the roof-ridge. Once there had been two chimneys, but the easterly one had been knocked down by a falling tree and as it only served a bed-room fireplace it had never been replaced. Matthew recalled his father saying of the cottage that it was, 'all odd, like a pig with one ear'.

Matthew saw Flint Hill in the distance, too, and was reminded that it was time to go home, so he called up Jet, who had been inspecting Fielding's sheep with a professional eye, and they went back to the Landrover. She jumped in beside him, unable to take her usual place at the back since they had loaded the timber. She had not been quite sure about the unaccustomed honour of sitting in the passenger seat at first, but now she had grown quite cocky about it, and sat up, proud as a visiting duchess. She turned her head towards him, the white triangle gleaming between her eyes: the Trig-mark. He would always miss Trig, he knew that, but there was no ache in it now.

'If you're ready, your Ladyship,' he said, 'I'll drive you home.'

CHAPTER 7

The year moved on and Matthew's rebuilding progressed. He worked with slow ease, enjoying himself. He took pleasure in building, his muscles well attuned to the work, and the materials and tools to hand. It was akin to the satisfaction he got from drawing, except that this was a more physical thing. He would look at the stacked wood, new and gleaming, with a pleasantly anticipatory tension in his body, and his hand would be about the smooth handle of his saw in his imagination, moments before it was in fact, while his eye sized up the job to be done and the pattern of the timber in the construction.

Jet did not like it when he worked on the roof. She would try to climb a few rungs of the ladder to be near him, but she could not get a proper purchase on the rounded wood and her forearms ached when she tried to hook herself on. She could hear that he was cheerful enough though, hammering away. She would have to be content with that. He called down to her reassuringly, aware of her anxiety.

'I'll be down soon, don't you fret. We'll pull this place together by its own bootstrings, you'll see, little bitch.'

The day the tractor-shed roof was finished was Sam Hallett's last day's work at Fishers' yard. A bigger concern had opened up not far away and swallowed the little business whole. Hallett was lucky: he had been offered a job there, while a good many would go on the dole, but lucky or not, he was going to miss Fishers' after all the years he had worked there. Near enough fifteen years, since he had gone round there, cap in hand, the day after he left school.

He looked all round the timber-yard. It was odd, but it already had the look of dereliction about it. The stacks of wood, the saws and their benches had all gone and nothing moved but the grey dog pacing the length of his chain. Well, Sam had his orders about that. He was to take the dog out into the country and shoot it. He had said that was what should be done with the animal so many times, but now he had got the job himself he wished there were some way out of it. He had to admit though that there was nothing else to be done with such an unreliable brute, and the boss would not waste good money paying a vet to put him down, so Sam was lumbered.

He got into the van and backed it quite close to where the dog stood. There was a wire-mesh grille across the back that made a compartment in which the animal could safely travel. Sam opened the back doors and then held up to the Alsation, in plain sight but well out of reach, a chunk of raw meat the boss had left for the purpose. The dog had not eaten all day and he slavered excitedly at the prospect of food. Then Sam, with deliberately slow action, tossed the meat into the back of the van so that the dog would have leapt after it if it had not been for the chain. Then, sure that the dog would be more attentive to the meat than to him, he went quickly to release the other end of the chain from the post to which it was attached and the Alsation sprang into the van after the meat, with the chain trailing behind him.

Sam tossed the end of the chain in after his captive and slammed the doors, relieved to have that job over. In his opinion he could have shot the dog here and now in the yard, but the boss thought there might be complaints, or they would have the police round at the sound of a shot, or some busybody might try to interfere and get bitten for his pains. So Sam got into the driver's seat and drove out of the yard for the last time, his passenger growling and snarling in the back over his unexpected meal.

It was a bright, brisk day and Sam tried hard to forget the purpose of his journey, as far as anyone could, cooped up in the van with those great teeth no distance at all from his neck. He whistled a bit to cheer himself up, and looked around him as far as attention to the road would allow. He had lived in Clipton all his life and he liked the countryside that surrounded it. He brought the wife and kids out at week-ends for a picnic and a breath of air. Good air and wide spaces. It was great: good to look at even now, with winter stripping the trees and taking the colour from the fields. It would not be long before Christmas. Now, what would that boy of his want this time? A train set? Spacemen? Ruth wanted a pony, of course, but how was he supposed to manage that on his wages, and anyway, where could they possibly keep it? There was not even room for a rabbit on the Halletts' lawn, let alone a pony. Well, one thing was for sure, he would not be taking this fellow in the back home for them as a Christmas pet.

His eyes were on the road, but only half his attention, for the way ahead was dead straight for a mile or so along this stretch, where it followed the course of an old Roman marching route that strode unwavering to the horizon. It was only a minor road now and Sam had met no traffic for a quarter of an hour or so. He felt relaxed and cheerful, thinking to himself about Christmas, and was taken entirely by surprise when there was a sharp report as if a gun had gone off, and the van shuddered violently. For a fraction of a second Sam wondered if his shotgun had by some terrible mischance fired itself, but then came the diagnostic, rhythmic thudding that follows a blown tyre. He stopped and got out. The rear offside tyre spread out like a duck's foot under the wheel, with the van resting its weight on it as if suddenly weary. Sam swore. Then he swore again as he remembered where the jack was. It was in the back of the van with the dog.

Sam leaned against the wing of the van and considered the situation. They were well out in the country and in a lonely spot. The road's main function was to link a handful of isolated farms and houses. Come the snow it was always one of the first in the area to get blocked. He had taken the route particularly, to find a quiet place for the job in hand, so perhaps fate had chosen this very spot.

He took the shotgun out of the van and loaded it. He laughed at himself for having allowed his mind to think for one moment that he would have driven along with it armed. He put it on safety and went to let the dog out. The moment he jumped down, clear of the van, Sam planned to shoot him. He pressed down on the door-handle and stood back. The dog uncurled himself and looked about, puzzled. He had not been out of the yard for so long that he felt unsure of himself in these new surroundings, and the jolting of the van had made the rapidly chewed meat sit uncomfortably in his stomach. Still, many new smells came to him on the wind and some of them stirred his blood strangely. The wet, black nose quested about and the grey ears pricked alertly. The dog lowered himself to the ground with caution and the chain came clanking after him. Sam reached for the gun which he had set against the wing of the van, but the dog saw the move he made and, knowing a threat when he saw one, the Alsation acted in an instant, lunging past Sam quicker than Sam could move to stop him, and the flying chain caught Sam's ankle such a blow that he was knocked over by the force and the pain of it. He got to his feet again quickly, his ankle hurting so fiercely that water stood in his eyes. He raised the gun and fired, but it was only at a flying shadow that he fired, and the noise of the shot echoed emptily round him.

'Damn that dog to hell,' he said. What was he to do now? He would never find him again in all this open country. He swallowed his conscience and told himself the animal would not last long; he could not fend for himself: some farmer was bound to see him and shoot him or he would get caught up on that chain and be hanged.

Sam got out the jack and the spare

wheel and rolled up his sleeves.

At Pennant Farm, Peggy Davey was icing the Christmas cake. The puddings, made weeks ago before Stir-up Sunday, stood in their cloth caps on the larder shelf. Peggy had nieces and nephews in large numbers and they would all come to her table at some time over the festival. She enjoyed this. It made the house come alive.

She was glad that Ellen had decided to come after all. Ellen was her youngest sister, an afterthought really, when Ma had considered she had put all that sort of thing behind her. She had been an odd child, their Ellen—bright, wayward, behaving sometimes like a spoilt brat, though she was never overindulged in practice, with three older sisters, and a brother, as well as Ma and Pa to keep her in order—but she had shrugged out from under them somehow, their authority running off her like rain off a roof. It was the same at school. 'Brilliant, but will not accept discipline,' her reports had said.

Peggy remembered the look on Ma's face when Ellen had announced that she was pregnant, the day before her seventeenth birthday: remembered her own feelings too, married some time, and urgently hoping for babies of her own, and the thought stirring almost at once in the back of her mind that perhaps they could keep the whole thing quiet and let Peggy take the baby when it was born and say it was her own. It had seemed more important than Ellen's defiant distress and had made Peggy ashamed of herself.

Ellen had had her own plans though. She and her young man Peter were to be married and, rather to everyone's surprise, he had agreed to it. He was a charming enough young fellow, but footloose and with not much taste for being tied down, so he must have been properly taken with Ellen at the beginning, to have gone through with it.

Give Ellen her due though, once she had married him, she had stuck to him and tried to make a go of it. Her wildness had channelled itself into intense devotion to her children: Steve, the oldest, Anna, conceived almost before Ellen had had time to take breath after the first, and then, after some false starts, the second daughter, Sarah, who would be ten in the New Year. It was as well Ellen had Sarah. Anna had been killed, only a few months ago, in a road accident. Ellen's incredible calmness and courage when it happened had amazed Peggy. Somehow you always expected people close to you to remain the same, and her picture of Ellen was always of a wild young girl, temperamental, obstinate, emotional. She had watched Ellen at the funeral and marvelled at her dignity. It had been her husband, Peter, who had broken down at the graveside. Afterwards, though, Ellen had come to Peggy and held on to her tight, as if she were the last rock visible in a flood. She had said nothing and Peggy had not dared to. There had been no tears, just the two of them, close, taking comfort from each other. Peggy found her eyes were wet, just remembering it. She knew Ellen had been hurt more and more since then, as Peter found his own way to salve his wounds, mostly with the aid of any pretty young woman who was willing. He would turn up for Christmas, Peggy expected, if only for the look of the thing, but at least it would be good for Sarah and Steve to have their Dad around.

Peggy plunged the icing set into the washing-up bowl, swished the plastic pieces about and watched the fragile rainbow bubbles of froth on the water forming and shifting and re-forming. John Davey came into the kitchen, sniffing appreciatively at the rich cooking-smells. He came up behind her and put his arms round her waist.

'You were looking thoughtful,' he said.

She laughed. 'How could my back view look thoughtful?' she asked him.

'It's a well known view,' he said. 'I know you from all angles, my old love, and you were looking thoughtful. What were you thinking?'

'Life is like a washing-up bowl full of bubbles.'

'Good God, woman, that sounds like a cross between Patience Strong and a telly commercial. Get on with your cooking and leave philosophy to the experts.'

'Don't you be saucy to me, John Davey, or I'll not make any toffee. The afternoon's almost gone as it is.'

John Davey liked Peggy's home-made toffee not so much for itself, though he enjoyed a piece now and then, as for the fact that it took a deal of eating, being the sort that tended to glue the teeth together, and that kept the kids quiet from time to time.

By tea-time everything was done and put away. Peggy had set one or two things aside for Matthew and a small pudding too. Goodness knows if he would eat it. Most likely he would share it with that dog of his, but there was no one else to bake for him, and she would not have him setting aside the season altogether. She would walk up there later and take it to him and see if he felt like talking for a while. He was healing slowly, she knew that, from what she had heard from the men and from what little she had seen for herself, but he was still a lonely man who did not even realize that he was lonely. She checked herself. John would say she was interfering and perhaps he was right. Perhaps Matthew genuinely needed no company but that of his dog. It was easy enough to imagine that everyone needed love in the same form, to want to interfere with the fine balance of contentment, and Matthew seemed content enough. Yet he was not complete.

'You're an old busybody,' she scolded herself.

She took the pudding and the other Christmas stores to him all the same, and sat and talked to Matthew in his kitchen, telling him all her plans for the festivities. She wished he would let her tidy the place up a bit—it was a proper pig-sty—but she knew better than to suggest it. He seemed easier with her than he had been, and took her to see the new roof on the tractor shed. He had made a fine job of that. Jet walked with them and Peggy looked her over admiringly.

'She's a lovely dog, Matthew, a real credit to you. When I think how she lay out on that dung-heap, with us thinking she was dead...I'm glad you saved her, Matthew.'

He smiled slowly, and looked down at her. He did not hide his face from Peggy, he knew her too well.

'I'm glad too,' he said.

Peggy looked at him a while, and then said, 'Would you come to Christmas dinner with us, Matthew? The family will all be coming. You'd be very welcome.'

'It's kind of you,' he said, 'but I'll be fine here.'

He saw her to the gate, and then turned away to the house, putting his coat collar up to ward off the wind.

High up on the hill, the grey dog lay and panted. Since leaving Sam behind he had run a good mile before even so much as stopping to look around. Then he had trotted on at a slower pace until the trailing chain had wedged itself fast in the undergrowth and the dog was once more held secure by the leather collar and the iron links. For an hour or more he had tugged and struggled, and now lay exhausted. It was a long time since he had eaten the meat, and he had not stopped for water, so now he was hungry and thirsty too, with no prospect of release. There was little light left and the air was growing very cold. A few feather-like flakes of early snow came with a rising wind and the Alsation shivered. Then, turning his back to the wind, he curled nose to tail, sighed, and disposed himself to sleep, for if he could not change his situation, then he must endure it. Life in the yard had taught him that lesson.

Some hours later, the fox came trotting up the hill, with head held high so that his thieving paws should not trip over the trailing wing of the splendid fat cockerel he carried. The hen-houses at

Flint Hill and Pennant having proved impregnable, he had gone further along the hill to a house where there was no dog and where the hens were sometimes not shut in at night, their owner having spent too long at the Dog and Partridge. The cockerel had squawked defiance at him, but not for long.

The Alsation, waking from a sleep troubled by dream-huntings in which his prey perpetually eluded him, smelt the harsh smell of the fox. He smelt the cockerel too, all warm and bloody, and the saliva flowed in his mouth.

The fox seemed to leer as he went past and a real ferocity arose in the grey dog, who threw himself, howling, to the end of the chain with such force that the leather collar, against which he had struggled for so long, burst its stitches and fell away.

The fox had dodged many dogs in his life and he had been hunted once, too; had lain in the low branches of a willow tree and watched hounds casting about by the stream below, foiled and fooled.

But now a dark ancestral terror took hold of him at the sight and sound of the gaunt grey creature that had sprung out of the trees: the ancient fear of the wolf seemed to melt his bones, and he dropped his kill and bolted, heading for his earth as fast as his red legs would take him there. Better hungry than dead.

The Alsation nosed at the bright feathers of the cockerel, and then he pulled out a mouthful or so to get at the flesh. The feathers stuck to his lips and tongue and made him gag, but at last he got the trick of avoiding them and lay down content to tear the meat and crunch the bones.

The Pennant hens roosted safe and secure, talking soft hen-talk to each other as they dozed. They had heard the fox about, scratching at the woodwork, sniffing at the door-jamb, but he had gone away again, disappointed. In a pen across the yard the Christmas turkey slept too, but her security would only be short-term. Tomorrow John Davey would bring home a tree from Enstone

Copse for the children to decorate when they came. Tomorrow the turkey would hang in the Pennant larder.

John Davey stirred in his sleep, for it was almost time to be up. Half in dream and half awake, he thought back over the year. It had been a good harvest, thank the Lord, and a peaceful back end to set the place to rights before growth started again. Like riding a roundabout that never stopped, that's what farming was. Plough and grow and harvest and store, and take a quick breath and plough again. Now he had woken to a brisk day by the sound of it. There was a high wind coming off the hill. That would bring snow with it, coming from that direction.

'It's a great life if you don't weaken,' he said aloud.

'What's that you said?' Peggy was awake and looking at him sleepily. She still looked hardly more than a girl when she first woke, tousled and pink with sleep.

'I thought I must be getting old,' John Davey said. 'But I'm not sure I am now.'

Lights shone in the kitchen at Flint Hill as Matthew got ready for milking. It was still black dark outside and there was more than a handful of snow in the wind. He watched the flakes starring themselves on the glass of the window-panes, and he reached for his thick coat. There was a real wind blowing as he stepped out of the house, roaring in the trees like a thundering train, forcing the breath back into his body. Jet's light frame leaned into it and it blew back her silky hair and flattened her ears to her head. The roaring made her uneasy, but there was something else that stirred her, that twitched her nerve-ends. Matthew felt it too, and his neck hairs prickled as the wind carried down to them the sound of a high and mournful howling.

CHAPTER 8

Shepley made the most of Christmas. The Sunday school celebrated in a welter of stammering shepherds and plump angels whose heraldic messages were full of conviction, if somewhat out of tune. The Dog and Partridge got in extra beer and supplies of such drinks as rum and créme de menthe, which it never normally stocked but which sold with alacrity over the festive season as wives and mothers and aunts boldly celebrated where they would normally never set foot. The Dog and Partridge was not a woman's pub, but Christmas was Christmas, after all.

For tradition's sake, Matthew picked a branch of holly from the hedge and hung it up in the kitchen, and on Christmas day he cooked an old fat hen for himself and Jet. He had grown used to looking after himself and was quite handy in the kitchen. What might look a muddle to anyone else was a kind of order to him, for he knew where everything was that he was likely to need. Despite this self-reliance though, he always accepted with grace the offerings that Peggy brought him from her own kitchen, and he had set the pudding she gave him to simmer on top of the stove. He had even scalded himself some cream to go with it. He was glad he had seen a little more of Peggy lately. Thwarted of mothering her own, she had mothered him since he was tiny. Mothered every other creature that stood in need of it, too, and to reject her kindness would have been to reject the breast. He would not go to Pennant today, though. It would be as full of people as a marketplace and he would rather just have Jet's company. He made that clear to everyone.

When he and Jet had eaten and treated themselves to a snooze by the fire, he went out into the yard, for there was work to be done and the daylight hours were at their shortest. The snow had not come to much, but there was a sprinkling of it on the cobbles, and on the sunless side of the wall there was a thin film of ice. The sky was solid grey cloud, with plenty more snow to come. It would settle if it fell now.

Then he heard the sound of hoofbeats.

'Damn me,' he said to Jet. 'She's here again.'

He looked hard and deliberately at the girl as she rode up to him. She could have a good sight of his face. That might put her off coming this way, making a nuisance of herself. She only looked directly back at him, though, and smiled and said, 'Happy Christmas.'

'And the same to you,' he said, deliberately ungracious.

She looked very brown, Matthew thought. It must be all that expensive sunshine. Mind you, the heat must have affected her, for she was a deal thinner, and she had not been plump before. For a moment he thought of Patty's generous body. Good enough to eat, he used to tell her. Well, he was not moved by the thought of it now. That was history.

He raised a hand to Mary West as she rode on by, enough to acknowledge her visit without showing the least pleasure in it. She looked a fine sight though, he had to admit that, with the cold making her tanned skin glow. Still he found her confident friendliness irritating. It could be arrogance, after all, that brightness of eye that made you look at her. You could not ignore her, though, even if you wanted to, for there was a presence about her, that indefinable quality that makes one fine beast gain the prize from another in the ring or in the stockyard.

God, that would take her down a peg or two, if she knew he had been sizing her up like a heifer or a ewe. He grinned to himself at the thought. He wondered, vaguely, about this property she had come into. One of the village houses perhaps. Nice to inherit money at her age, especially when you were well-heeled already. He walked back indoors, to his own inheritance, and threw his coat on the table. He felt restless and unseasonably irritable and he would have to calm himself down a bit before milking. The cows always knew if he were out of temper and it affected their yield. There were people who would think he was daft to say so, now the milking was all by machines, which could not express mood through their manipulation of the teats as a hand-milker would, but it was true for all that.

So he fetched an old pipe that had not seen the light of day for a good many months and filled it full of the rich dark tobacco that John Davey had given him. He sat by the fire and puffed away at it till it drew.

'Come here, Jet,' he called.

She had been sitting on the window-sill, watching the snow beginning to fall again, and she jumped down and came to sit by him, pressed hard against his thigh with her wise head in his lap. She sighed a deep dog-sigh of content to be with him. She gave him all he asked of her, and demanded nothing, yet she was a free spirit, and no slave.

'You'll do,' he said.

Outside, creatures huddled in earths and hollows, in the lee of rocks and trees, out of the snow and the biting wind. Hedgehogs, little spiked urchins, rolled up in leaves and soft earth, slept away the winter months. It was the hungry season, when the autumn's seeds and berries had been stripped and nothing new had yet dared to grow, so you slept, or you hoarded, or you stole from man, who had plentiful stores kept for his own selfish use. But if you were careless he trapped you and killed you, and if you escaped him, you stood in danger of being caught by some creature even hungrier then yourself and with a taste for meat.

Mary West came cantering back home through the woods, her jacket huddled round her, her hands thrust under her horse's mane, trying to keep warm, for her fingers were numb in spite of her gloves. She would not exchange this for the hot sun she had left behind, but she wished the weather had not turned so bitter so quickly, before she had had time to become acclimatized.

She felt the bay horse tremble under her hand.

'What's the matter, Laurel?' she asked him.

He was tensed up beneath her and it was not with cold. He snorted and began to dance and the veins stood out on his skin. Something moved among the trees and he shied so violently that she was nearly unseated.

'You silly fellow,' she said, soothing him. 'It was only a dog,' and calmed by her voice, he cantered on steadily into the dusk.

At Pennant, Peggy Davey sat, happily weary, among her brood of nieces and nephews. Sarah and Steve seemed cheerful enough, though she could have wished their father had been more relaxed with them. If ever there were a man on a duty visit, it was Peter. Still, it had given Ellen a chance to rest and eat a good meal someone else had cooked and be looked after a bit. It might seem silly, but Peggy still looked on Ellen as a child, and as much in need of a treat. She looked so happy now, flushed by the warmth from the logs in the hearth, playing a scandalously cheating game of Ludo with her children, but Peggy had seen the tautness in her face when she had arrived and the over-bright smile that was so uncharacteristic of her.

In the kitchen, John Davey was, by tradition, doing the washing up. He only did it once a year and he liked to be left alone to get on with it. He clattered about among the day's mountain of crockery and smiled to himself. His old Peg had done it again, had made Christmas a day out of time, as it should be.

The rector, who had preached to a good-sized congregation that morning, walked through the bitter gloom to say Evensong to an empty church. By now they would all have forgotten what it was all about again, and tomorrow it would be hangovers and indigestion pills, but he supposed the Lord must be used to it, after all these hundreds of years. He lit the altar candles and their lights pricked out like small stars.

' "Good deeds in a naughty world",' he said. He thought to himself he must go up and see Matthew Ratton. He did not find it easy to talk to the man, but he really must try. After all, they were both experts on the behaviour of sheep.

CHAPTER 9

There was a drift of whiteness over the woods above Tally Cottage. Matthew noticed it as he came down across Wally Field with Jet at his heels. He had to look twice to see if it were smoke or mist. Sometimes the trees would gather great swirls of mist about themselves, and it would seem that the whole woodland was on fire, but this time it was genuine smoke. He walked along the field a way to where there was a clearer view of the cottage below and then he could see that the smoke rose from the chimney- harmless, domestic smoke that formed a pillar at first in the cold air, and then drifted away to curl itself about the trees. Well, at least he was assured that the place had not caught fire, but someone must be in the cottage, which had been empty for years and was in a bad state.

It could well be that a passing tramp had shouldered in the rotten hinges and was making himself comfortable for a day or so on his travels. Matthew had nothing against tramps, but if a fire were left unattended in the cottage it could spread quickly enough even in winter and not only finally ruin the cottage but damage the woodland as well. What if it were a genuine tenant though? Could that mean the hill grazing had been spoken for while he had been dithering about it? He hoped not.

He decided he had better go down and see what was going on, but first he must look at Charity. The little heifer was due to calve soon. She had been one of a set of triplets that Peggy had determinedly reared for Dan Ratton when the old cow Rose had died producing them. Faith, Hope and Charity, Peggy had named them. Triplets rarely flourished, but these did, and grew into three splendid animals. Faith and Hope had since been sold on, but Charity had joined the herd and would have her first calf soon. She was a nice little heifer, prettily marked, and with a temperament to match her name.

She turned her head as Matthew came in to see her. She stood in deep straw, her belly enormous, but she seemed quite content and comfortable. Matthew scratched the hard ridge of her head and talked to her softly for a while. Jet lay quietly in a corner so as not to disturb her.

'She's not ready just yet. I can leave her a while, Jet, while we see what's going on at Tally Cottage. Come on now.'

They walked together along the track that led into the woods. There was a clear sky overhead and a wintry sunlight washed the fields. High up over the woods a buzzard wheeled and turned in slow, lazy circles, fingering the air. It was a deceptive laziness, though. Once he had prey in sight he would drop swift as a stone. They were beautiful birds and Matthew was glad to see them increasing. They had been rare enough a few years back when poison sprays were the fashion of the day and no one had thought enough of the long-term results of them. So poisoned seeds poisoned the mice who in their turn poisoned the birds of prey or made their eggs sterile and useless.

Soon the man and his dog plunged into the woodland. There were plantations at first of larch and fir, the larches like skeletons and seemingly as dead, the firs making their own gloom as they hid their trunks from the daylight. Matthew did not like the conifers and was glad to come out into the old woodland beyond, where ash and beech stood tall over them; no age at all really, as a tree reckons it, but older than Matthew and stretching up like pillars on either hand.

Though he was walking for a purpose —for he seldom had leisure to go for walks just for their own sake, to scuffle his boots through the soft leafmould under the great trees as he had done with such delight when he was a boy, unearthing as he went treasures of conkers or beech-mast or oakapples, and watching startled mice and darting insects scurry away from his feet—Matthew felt in a holiday mood, and he picked up a stick and threw it for Jet. She knew what he expected, but was puzzled by the levity in him. She was his workmate and life was too serious for play. She had put that behind her with puppyhood. Only for a moment did she pause, though, and then she was off, to find the stick and to fetch it back. He threw it again and again she fetched it, and he gave her a great clouting caress that made her bark with delight. Poor little bitch. She didn't get much fun. She deserved better. Matthew watched her gambolling about in the undergrowth and made up his mind that he would let her compete in the trials, come summer, however much he disliked the idea for himself. It would be a busman's holiday, fair enough, but he felt she would enjoy the sense of occasion, and if she did well it would be all to her credit, and if she did not, it would be Matthew's fault, not hers.

They arrived at the gate of Tally Cottage. A track led down from the top road, but that was its only access, its only connection with other houses, other people, unless those people cared to walk through the woods as Matthew had done. It stood quite alone in its small garden, surrounded by woodland on three sides, and on the other the steep rough grass rose up behind it. The derelict remains of the old lambing pens spilled down this hillside and it seemed it would not be long before the cottage was in a similar state. There was a large fenced enclosure on the hillside beyond the garden wall, too, and the hurdles that formed the fence were slowly rotting away, but by the entrance to this paddock were several tall posts, worn smooth as ships' masts by age and weather, and on these had been notched the seasonal count of sheep, by generations of shepherds who could count only by the numbers of their fingers and who had had no letter-learning at all. They would mostly have been good shepherds, for all that. A damned sight better than Tom Fielding, Matthew reckoned.

With his hand on the gate, Matthew suddenly wondered what he was going to say if someone answered the door of Tally Cottage. A tramp would make a quick exit through the back on hearing a knock, but what could he say to a bona fide occupier? 'I thought the cottage might be on fire'? It obviously was not. 'I'm your nearest neighbour'? He did not wish to be saddled with being neighbourly. He began to think better of having come at all and was about to turn away when the door opened. Framed against the gloom of the cottage interior, covered in dust and cobwebs and carrying a large plastic bucket was Mary West.

'What are you doing here?' Matthew said.

It sounded ruder than even he would have intended. After all, she could equally well ask him that question. He flushed and looked down at his boots, feeling cloddish and very stupid, and angry with himself for feeling so.

'Please, come in,' she said, and walked down the path to open the gate for him.

'Saw smoke,' he muttered. 'Wondered if everything was all right.'

'I was burning rubbish in the end fireplace,' she said. 'I'm getting the cottage ready to live in. It's mine now, you know.'

'Oh,' said Matthew. Any other words he may have had in his head seemed to have left him high and dry. He could say nothing at all, but stood, neither coming nor going.

'I was left it by an eccentric great-aunt,' Mary explained. 'She was a suffragette and refused to let a man inherit her property as a protest against women not having the vote, so it was left in trust until a suitable female relative could be found. Our family goes in for boys a great deal and I was the first available female of direct descent, so now it's mine. It's been mine since I was twenty-one, in fact, but I've been too occupied with other things to claim it before now, and the poor old place is in a worse state than I'd realized.'

Matthew gazed round him, nodding agreement. She would have her work cut out putting the cottage in order. He wondered what she would do about the land. He wanted to ask her, so much so that it burned indigestibly inside him, but he could not get the words out. He stood and stared all around her, so as not to be caught staring *at* her. He wished she would say something that would give him the office to go. Even he had to admit that he had already been quite sufficiently ungracious.

'I'd ask you in for some tea,' she said, 'but I've no supplies here and I've drunk what I had in the thermos to lay the dust.'

'I'll be away anyway,' Matthew said, relieved. 'I only came to see there was nothing wrong. I won't bother you any longer.'

He turned quickly and walked away. Jet, who had been lying near the gate, rose to her feet and trotted after him.

'Thank you for taking the trouble. It was kind of you,' the girl called out. There was no hint of irony in her voice but he knew she much be mocking him. It must have been obvious to her that he had intended her no kindness. All his earlier elated mood had vanished and now he walked the woods and scarcely saw them. The last thing he wanted was that girl permanently on his doorstep whenever she was not gadding off abroad. Jet drooped miserably, feeling his anger and wondering if in some way she were the cause of it.

All the rest of the morning the black mood was on him and thoughts churned wordlessly and uselessly in his head. He knew the sheepwalks went with the cottage. They always had done: there would be no changing that. Once Fielding's lease was up they would be at her disposal.

So it would be up to her to lease them or use them as she thought fit. He'd be damned if he'd go crawling to her for the lease. Let her play shepherdess for a bit and perhaps she would be glad enough to be rid of the responsibility. After all, she could hardly do the sheep much more harm than had been done already. Round and round went the thoughts in his mind and he could not seize on one that made him feel better, unless it were that the inheritance he had imagined for her—some neat, prosperous little place in a well-tended garden—was so ludicrously unlike the reality. That thought alone allowed him some malicious amusement.

When he had eaten his meal and fed Jet, he went out to the cowhouse to look at Charity and was promptly shaken out of himself by what he saw. She had been fine enough when he looked in just before having his bite to eat, lowing softly to herself in the initial discomfort of labour, but now she was contracting hard and when he had stayed and watched her for a while he could see that all her effort was not shifting the calf at all. If she had been a mare he would have sent for the vet at once, but a cow can endure a more protracted labour, with no harm done to herself and the calf, as long as nothing is wrong inside. This he must find out, and the sooner the better.

Matthew stripped off his jacket and soaped his arm in the bowl of warm water had had ready, to feel inside her for the source of any trouble. The vet would be a needless expense if he could put matters right himself.

He could feel the forefeet of the calf, nicely presented, so it was coming the right way, and he could feel no other feet. The thing he dreaded most was finding a tangle of twin calves to be sorted out, but he was pretty certain this was a singleton. His fingers searched for the calf's nose which should follow the forefeet in a nice, streamlined, easily-deliverable shape, but he could not feel a nose. Now he knew what the trouble was. The head was turned back on the calf's shoulder, as if it wished to look back into the womb, and so the heifer's contractions could not push it out. Had she been a roomy cow, Matthew could have turned the head with little trouble, but when he tried it with Charity he soon realized that the passage was too small and his hands too large.

Many men, to save the expense of the vet, would have roped the calf there and then and dragged it into the world, somehow, but Matthew did not want to lose Charity or the calf.

There had never been a phone at Flint Hill. He crossed the yard to the Landrover. It would not start. He got out and flung open the bonnet, glaring furiously at the aged engine that had chosen this moment to let him down.

Hoofs clattered across the yard. A voice said, 'Hello.' It was Mary West. 'There was something I should have asked you when I saw you at the cottage,' she said, 'but it only occurred to me when you'd gone. Still, that can wait. What's wrong? You look as though you need help.'

Matthew snapped at her. 'Everything's

bloody wrong.' He would have to ask her. There was no help for it.

'Could you ride down to Pennant for me? Ask them to send the vet. My heifer's in trouble, calving.'

She looked at him for a moment and then to his amazement she got off her horse, hitched him to the tie-ring by the trough and walked over to the cowhouse.

He stood stock-still, staring after her, and she turned and said, 'Show me.'

His amazement flared into anger. Why couldn't she do a simple thing when she was asked? Just ride down to Pennant and phone. It wasn't much to ask, though it had galled him to ask it.

'What the hell do you think you're doing?' he shouted, furious with her. 'You're not a bloody vet, are you?'

'No,' she said coolly. 'I'm not a bloody vet, but show me. Perhaps I can help.'

By now he felt too astounded to argue further, but showed her into the calving box where Charity was. Mary spoke briefly to the heifer and ran her hands over her swollen belly. Then she stripped off jacket and sweater. She had on a sleeveless T-shirt under this. He was staring at her.

'Quite respectable, you see,' she said. 'Where's your soap and water?' He pointed to the bowl and she scrubbed her hands and arms briskly, so that even under her tan the skin grew pink. Then she laughed. 'Well,' she said, 'there's a first time for everything.'

Matthew could have hit her. If he had dared leave her alone with Charity he would have ridden that horse himself down to Pennant to phone the vet. He was no equestrian, but he would just about stay on. If she was going to muck about with his heifer, he was damned if he would warn her what would happen if the animal strained while she had her arm inside. Break it for her, probably. That was always supposing she intended putting her arm in the heifer anyway. Perhaps she had some other method in mind. Soothe her fevered brow and exhort her to be brave perhaps. God help us, he thought.

Mary West felt carefully inside Charity and located the source of the trouble.

'Bad presentation,' she said. 'She's small, isn't she?'

'Aye,' said Matthew, astounded at her.

'Hold her tail, will you. I'll feel about a bit more.' He held the tail. Her face was intent, concentrated, as if trying to establish the combination of an unknown safe. He felt she had forgotten he was there. At last she said, 'I think I can get the head right. My hands are smaller than yours. Can you stop her going down till I've finished? She's not steady on her feet. I can feel it.'

'I won't let her go down,' Matthew said, 'if you think you can do it.'

'Skinny arms,' she said. 'It'll save you time and money. Think of that.' She gave him a look that he could not quite decipher and held out her unoccupied arm for his inspection. Slender enough to work better in a small space than his own brawny ones.

He was not sure whether he nodded his assent or not, but she seemed to think he did for she continued to work. She talked quietly, to herself, to Charity; not, recognizably, to him.

Once she said, 'Natural childbirth, my foot,' and grinned. Then at last she said, 'I think that's got it,' and almost as she said it, almost as if Charity knew that now her efforts would not be wasted, the heifer contracted strongly, clamping down hard on Mary's arm. Up till now she had managed to withdraw and avoid the contractions, but this one had taken her unaware and she gasped and nearly fell. When it passed she withdrew her arm and stood back, and before long Charity made another tremendous effort, sending her calf out into the world to lie in a glistening heap on the straw. She turned, puzzled for a moment, and then by instinct began to lick away the slime.

'Good God,' Matthew said. 'You did it.'

He was crouched close behind her,

looking over her shoulder at the calf as she examined it. Her T-shirt was wet and patched with stains of muck and blood, and her arms were streaked with it. He was suddenly very much aware of the femaleness of her and for the first time in many months he felt his body stir and quicken. He was amazed, much as if a stone had flowered. He was damned if he would give her the satisfaction of knowing she had aroused him, though. He turned away and plunged his arms to the elbow in the cold water in the water-bucket. Daft, boy-scout sort of thing to do, he thought, but after a while it quietened the tumult of his body. He was not going to let himself lust after a woman he did not even like, even if she had delivered his calf for him; and it was a heifer calf too.

She came over and put her hand on his arm, and he jumped as if the hand were electric. She looked hard at him. Did she know? To hell with it. His face was flushed, like a schoolboy's. He could feel it, and the skin of his scars pulsed with

with the rush of blood. What a fool she had made of him: unwittingly perhaps, but she had.

'It's a heifer calf,' she said. Did she think he was blind or stupid?

'Yes,' he said. Then, grudgingly, 'Thank you.'

'I don't charge extra for heifer calves,' she told him. 'Come to think of it, I don't charge at all, but a cup of tea would be very welcome, if you can spare one.'

He did not want to take her into the house. It was his place, not the sort of which women approved. Still, he could hardly deny her some refreshment after her efforts, so having satisfied himself that Charity and her calf were well settled together, he led the way into the kitchen.

She sat down by the fire, with Jet beside her. She did not offer to help, but watched him as he walked about the kitchen. Matthew looked covertly at her too, wondering now, more objectively, what had caused that sudden, physical response to her. She was too thin and her brown hair was straight and heavy, caught back at the nape of the neck, making her face look even bonier than ever. It was an uncluttered face. The eyes that looked out of it were large and grey. She was not the least bit pretty, if Patty's face was the criterion of prettiness, so why in spite of himself did he find himself drawn to look at her? He suddenly had the thought that she had not had her hair done in London when she went. It was just as it was when he first saw her. Perhaps really expensive hairdressers' skill lay in concealing their art.

'Your arm OK?' he said.

'Fine,' she said. 'I'll have a bruise or so, but don't worry about it.'

He was amazed at how she had coped, and full of reluctant admiration. There was no question, she had known what she was at, but if she hoped he was going to ask for the story of her life she was mistaken. He did not suffer from such womanish curiosity. However she had come by her knowledge, he would be told sometime, by somebody. Whatever you wanted to know, Shepley would tell you eventually. He glanced across at her and felt the openness of her expression like an abrasion. Since the fire, he had become unused to being looked at. He had grown to expect the averted eye, especially from women. He felt uncomfortable. He brought her tea. He spoke of the weather. He felt very stiff, as if the last hour had never occurred, but she appeared to be unaware of this and seemed quite at home in his kitchen, with her arm round his dog's neck. His home's shortcomings in the matter of domestic hygiene and tidiness seemed to have escaped her notice.

'That was a good cup of tea. Thank you,' he said.

'Have some more.'

'No. I'll be off now. Laurel hates to be tied up for too long. Can I come back and see the calf in a day or two?'

'Yes,' said Matthew.

She walked to the door, turned and

hesitated for a moment, then said, 'I've been looking at your face. I know someone who could do a really good job on those scars if you wanted. But then, maybe you prefer not.'

Matthew felt as though he had been hit in the mouth. No one ever spoke to him about his face or drew attention to it and here she was, talking about it as if it were a wall in need of repair, a job of work for somebody. Unable to cope with the remark, he ignored it and went to open the door for her. Jet trotted after her, tail waving, eager to escort this friendly visitor to the gate. She approved of this person who smelt deliciously of horse and knew just where to scratch a dog behind the ears.

'You come back here,' Matthew shouted at her and she came back, puzzled that he should be so angry. Then, suddenly, Mary West was angry too.

'You've no reason to speak to the dog like that, Matthew Ratton. I believe you're jealous. Jealous because she knows I like her and has the good sense to see nothing wrong in that. I won't put her in danger of your short temper again. I hope the calf does well, but I won't be back to see her. I'm away again in a week's time, so you can walk your woods in peace. Goodbye.'

She crossed the yard, walking quickly, and untied the horse from the tethering-ring. She tightened the girth, gathered her reins and swung up into the saddle, all without a glance in Matthew's direction. The iron shoes clattered across the cobbles of the yard and out onto the track, where the sound was muted to a muffled thudding, as she pushed the horse on, first into a trot and then into a powerful, ground-devouring canter that soon had them well out of sight of Flint Hill.

Matthew turned and went to the cow-house and watched the new calf drinking from its mother. They would not stay together long, for the moment there was peace in the eager suckling and the heifer's gentle crooning. He could wish for such a peace. From time to time in his life he had felt it as part of himself, but now he was not sure that it would ever come again.

CHAPTER 10

The grey dog had wintered badly. The instinctive urge to hunt was strong in him, but he lacked skill and more often than not he would have to eat carrion or raid infrequent farmyard dustbins to get food. He grew thin and hungry and he wandered about, having no place in particular that he wanted to be; hating man and yet perplexed without him. Once he appeared out of a patch of scrub as a child was hurrying down the road to the school bus. He lifted his lips in a silent snarl and the child dropped its satchel and ran. There were sandwiches in the satchel and they took the edge off the dog's hunger.

Old Charley Bates looked along the line of the hedge and ditch with satisfaction—blackthorn staked and bound, and clean brown earth below for the field-drains to empty themselves along. He could still do a job well, seventy or no. A hundred yards or so away across the fields, the flail cutter had been along the lane and left the hazels all ripped and jagged, their branch ends a mess of wicked spears. It wasn't just that the old ways seemed best to an old man. Charley reasoned to himself. He had seen some good new things come to farming in seventy years: something approaching a decent wage to be had at last, and mucky, sweating work made easier by machinery, and about time, too. Still, he liked to see a job well done and to the purpose, and that flailed hedge would keep no stock in: they would have to put posts and wire behind it, and what was the point of fencing twice when once would do?

He looked again at his own hedge. No blundering cattle, no determined sheep would find a way through it, and if the hunt leaped it they would do it no harm nor themselves neither. God help any horse that straddled those hazel spikes the flail had left. Rip its guts out on the spikes, then tear itself to pieces on the wire, he wouldn't wonder.

Well, he had done a fair few hours. He'd sit down for a bite now. Smoke rose up sweetly from the fire of hedge-trimmings he had made at the field's edge, and he settled by it and took a swig of tea from his bottle. He had bread and cheese and pickles too, and he felt more than ready for them.

Then he was aware of quiet movement behind him, and turning his head, he saw that a grey dog had come up close and was watching him. Charley liked dogs and he chirruped to this one and held out a hunk of bread. The dog stepped forward, and then something in his eye made Charley cautious of offering bread from his hand. He put it down and the dog took it and swallowed it in one swift movement. Charley reached out for the packet of food, quite content to share it with this stranger, but the dog suddenly leaped and stood over it, snarling so savagely that the old man's heart began to thump and he wished he had not left his bill hook at the windward side of the hedge. There was something about this dog that proclaimed his snarling was no mere bluff. If Charley moved for the food, the dog would have him and no doubt about it. He sat as still as if he had grown roots, until the dog, still glaring at him, cold-eyed, clamped his jaws round the food-bag, then turned and trotted swiftly away.

'Well! Damn me!' exploded Charley, when his ungrateful visitor was far across the field.

It was not often the grey dog had such luck in the matter of food, though, and when the snow came he sheltered in a small cave up on the hill, with nothing more filling to eat than the odd beetle that he found there, so that when, one day after the thaw, he went loping down towards Tally Cottage, he was a walking hunger.

Ruth Hallet, out for a weekend walk with Sam and the others, had watched him come down through the gorse and the withered bracken, picking his way between hummocks of unmelted snow, and had tugged at her father's sleeve and said, 'Daddy! Daddy! I've seen a wolf. A real wolf!' Sam smiled and reassured her, but a thought stirred uncomfortably in the recesses of his mind.

The dog went snuffling about the doors of the cottage, but Mary was away and there was nothing about that he could eat. The bins and outhouses were empty. On the bank above the house a handful of ewes grazed on the sweet, snow-washed grass. They often came down to the lambing pens at this time of year, mainly because it was the most sheltered part of their hillside, but possibly too because for generations this had been where the ewes were brought for lambing, and sheep are creatures of custom.

One ewe, who had taken the ram early, too early by far for a hill flock, pawed at the grass and baaed softly. The lamb lay inside her, waiting to be born, head resting neatly on little blunt feet. She strained, bleated, champed on her cud and strained again. Finally she pushed the lamb out and turned to lick the membrane away from its face. The lamb sneezed and gave a shrill, gargling bleat as it took its first breath. The breeze carried the rich smell of the after-birth down to the grey dog as he stood in the Tally Cottage garden.

He found it and feasted on it, and after that he stayed with the flock, and with each early lamb he was there in attendance to eat the offal of birth, the discarded placenta.

Then a lamb was born dead and he ate that too, and then he realized that here was the best possible food-source of all.

Tom Fielding had not looked over his sheep for a week. It hardly seemed worth the trouble now the lease was to go to that young piece who had got Tally Cottage. Still, he might make some last minute profit out of a lamb or two. He was sitting by the fire in his house in the village. He stretched himself and felt the ache in his bones. An *anno Domini* ache, that was, he reckoned. Fielding was big-built and amiable-looking, but it was the amiability of the feckless man. He liked his comfort and his money's-worth better than he liked laying out his cash. He had not been a bad worker when he was a young man and under the eye of the old shepherd at Brierley, but since he had shepherded for himself, and the years had crept up on him, he had wanted life a bit easier.

He looked round the cluttered room in which he sat and pushed his dog away from the fire with his boot, for the collie sprawled half-way across the newspaper Fielding had let slip from his hands as he half-dozed. The dog jumped up and knocked over the teacup and plate that had been left at the edge of the hearth.

'Stupid bugger,' Fielding admonished it, aiming an unenthusiastic blow at its head. Better company than his wife, though. She would be at her sister's, he supposed. Time she came back and saw to the house a bit. He stuffed the newspaper under the cushion of his chair and stirred himself into fetching his coat and putting on his boots. He would drive over in the van and see how things were going. He had kept no account of when the ewes were due, but some of them might need bringing in closer to home. What that West woman would do with them when she took over he neither knew nor cared, but he would stick out for the sale-price of the lambs that were born under his tenancy. Only fair, that was. Anyway, that was what he had had to agree to when he took over from Jim Coggins all those years ago. Poor old Jim. Had his balls shot off in the war. Cut him clean as a whistle. He had heard things were almost as bad with Ratton up at Flint Hill. No go left in him at all since that fire. He had heard his Ellie and some of the village girls having a good giggle about it. Well, Ratton was not likely to get the sheepwalks off him now and he was glad. You could be too clever and think you knew too much. Ratton did for sure.

He drove up to the top of the hill and

began to look about for the sheep. His merle-coloured, wall-eyed dog Ben shed a bunch of them and brought them into a rough natural fold that the rocks made. Fielding looked them over and thought they would go a week or so yet, and set them free again.

Then he walked on down towards Tally Cottage with Ben at his heels, and he saw dead lambs on the hillside. He saw a ewe lying with her throat torn open and a great grey dog standing over her. Fielding only had his .22 with him. He had brought it to get a pigeon or so for the pot, or a couple of rabbits. It did not have the range or the power to kill the dog at that distance, but he raised it to his shoulder, nevertheless. That brute was too much for Ben to tackle, and anyway Fielding had no wish to sort out a fight.

The dog recognized the action and fled, the slug whanging harmlessly after him. Fielding watched him out of sight. Then he pushed at the body of the ewe with his foot. Killed her and half eaten her, that dog had. She must have tried to protect her lambs without success and then the dog had savaged her. God, what a size it was. Still, he had driven it off and would now take the rest of the flock back nearer home. Other shepherds must watch out for themselves, if the dog came near them.

The Alsatian ran a long way, frightened by the gun. Firearms were his only real fear. Even the rich supply of food he had found would not lure him back, so he returned to his carrion diet and the occasional unwary rabbit, and once, a cat that he found asleep on the sunny side of a wall, on one of the first mild days of the year.

The snowdrops and yellow aconites came and went, and the winter wheat pricked up green in orderly rows on the chocolate soil of the arable fields. There had been a late fall of snow, followed by a swift thaw, and the colours of the fields looked bright and strange when the snow had melted off them. John Davey was glad to see his land look so well. Mind you, so it should, with all the time and labour he put into it, let alone the fertilizers and the top quality seed and the thirsty, oil-consuming machinery.

Matthew kept a close eye on his ewes, heavy in lamb now, and Jet kept constant watch for anything that might disturb them. Strangers in the field, perhaps with a playful or a disobedient dog, could set them careering about and they might well lose their young. Flint Hill was too far from the town to have much trouble with pet dogs on the loose, but there had been a good many reports of sheep-worrying in the area, and Matthew hoped they would have none of that sort of trouble. Any dog could cause havoc with sheep, but a real sheep-worrier could destroy the flock. So often a confirmed sheep-worrier was a sheep-dog gone wrong: a professional that knew its business, but was using its skill to a bad end. It was not to be wondered at though, Matthew thought. To train a dog to work, you must use its old instincts as well as individual intelligence. To herd the flock is a hunting instinct. You round them up the easier to kill them. That's the point when your good dog's intelligence and devotion takes over and blocks the instinct to kill: but take away the devotion, unblock the old instinct, and your sheepdog becomes an expert murderer of sheep, with all the criminal requirements —motive, skill, opportunity.

Soon the grass would start to grow on the pastures near Flint Hill. Matthew liked to plan his lambs to come with the new grass. Perhaps they might not be ready for the early markets, but it saved on feed and with luck the weather was kinder. The biting cold and wet of many Februaries, he could remember, had been death to lambs.

The lambing pens stood ready. Built of hurdles and straw, they were put up each year in a different place and so organized that he had one field for the ewes in lamb and a nursery field where the young lambs and their mothers could graze after their few days in the pens. This field was one that had had no sheep on for a good long time and the grazing would be clean. There is a saying known to every shepherd that sheep's worst enemy is another sheep. Germs and parasites lurk in the land that is over-grazed and never rested. Matthew was never guilty of that. It was for the same reason that he moved his pens from year to year, so that there could be no build-up of infection in one place. He felt he would never be converted to lambing indoors, though many did it now, bringing their ewes into barns and sheds for the purpose of pumping their lambs with antibiotics to guard against joint-ill and naval-ill and all the other ills lamb-flesh is heir to. It made for a pleasanter life for the shepherd, mark you, for it was an uncomfortable business, walking the windy fields at night with a lantern, but Matthew would go on doing it until he could be convinced another way was better.

So winter retreated and growth began again and Shepley blossomed with new paint and early flowers and the bustle of spring cleaning. Washing could blow and billow on garden lines again instead of hanging wetly by the kitchen fire.

The grey dog had wandered a long way in the weeks that had brought winter to meet spring, and sometimes he had eaten well and sometimes he had gone hungry, but each lesson in his own survival that he learned, he learned well and profited by. And all the time his wanderings followed, as wanderings do, a vague circle —though a vast one, covering a great number of miles, so that reports of him came from many different places—and slowly the circle brought him round again until in late spring he came to Flint Hill and padded like a shadow along the track by the fields where Matthew's sheep were grazing. He was not hungry. He had learned to catch rabbits, which were more plentiful now, and there were rats and mice and small birds too, but at the sight of the flock a queer, irresistible excitement seized him, and he stood and watched with his jaws open and his tongue lolling over his teeth.

CHAPTER 11

That fine May evening, Matthew and Jet were eating supper in the kitchen. They had demolished between them the best part of a veal pie that Peggy had brought up from Pennant. She had spent a good while scolding him for not eating enough and not taking care of himself. She had put behind her now the terrible desire to pity him for his wrecked face and his solitary existence and had learned to accept these things as part of Matthew, and he in his turn allowed her almost as close as she once had been, and she was glad of the return of the old easiness.

They had walked the fields together in the late afternoon sunlight to look over the year's lamb-crop. Peggy knew a good deal about sheep, for her father had been a shepherd, and Matthew was pleased with her opinion that they were a good bunch. He thought so himself. He had had more ewe-lambs than wethers and had kept two splendid ram-lambs entire to sell on for breeding. What was more, even with most of his ewes twinning, he had only lost three lambs in all, which was not a bad total.

Tomorrow he would separate them from their mothers: it was time they were weaned off and many of the ewes would be glad of it. Their woolly babies were great strapping youths now, big enough to send their mothers staggering as they butted and pushed under them to get at the udder. They were a really strong lot and on good grazing they would do well and fetch a good price at market. Perhaps Flint Hill could really be said to be paying for itself again at last. It had been a battle all right, but at least there had been some minor victories. He had come right through the winter on his own hay, he had one or two nice calves to replenish the herd and all the re-building was complete. Now the grass showed promise of another good hay-harvest and he had eaten his first lettuce with Peggy's pie. He would plant out more cabbage tomorrow if he had a moment.

He saw then that Jet had got up from the rag-rug where she had been lying since supper and was walking up and down, as if restless.

'What's up?' he asked her.

She pricked her ears and concentrated her attention on something that she was aware of and he was not. Then, suddenly, she ran to the door and barked urgently. The hackles were well up on her back and she quivered with anxiety to be out.

Matthew opened the door for her and as he did so he heard the panicky bleating of sheep from the upper field. He grabbed his gun and he and Jet ran up the slope towards the ewes and lambs. Now he could hear, among the bleating, the sound of a terrible, savage growling that made his heart plummet, and his legs seemed to move as they do in a nightmare, bursting with effort but making no headway.

When he reached the field at last, he found the sheep milling about in the twilight, hysterical with fright, crashing into the walls as if blind as they tried to escape from their own terror, for now there was no dog to be seen. Several of the ewes lay torn and dead and one or two were prostrate and gasping for breath with glassily rolling eyes. Many others Matthew could see had blood on them and there were tufts of wool everywhere.

His feelings at the moment were inexpressible. Anger rose up in him, so hot that he almost choked, but he caught enough breath to send Jet out to gather the sheep. It was the hardest job she had ever been asked to do, but she was patient, so that gradually the panic left them and they knew her and let themselves be gathered up, to stand heaving and panting in the angle of the wall. Meanwhile Matthew looked over the injured and the dead. Some of the injured ones might recover, with luck. He would have to fetch the Landrover and carry them down in that.

Leaving Jet to guard the others, he drove the unharmed sheep down to the yard, wishing Jet could be in two places at once. But the sheep were exhausted and subdued, seeming glad to reach the safety of the farm, where he shut them up in the old bull pen.

He drove back to the field and looked over his losses. There were five ewes dead and two beyond recovery, but two ewes and two lambs who lay panting with fright were salvable, and he loaded them up and drove them down to the house. The dead would have to wait, and the two on the point of death. That left one lamb still unaccounted for. Matthew put the injured sheep in a stable and shut the door on them. They would have to be dressed and stitched if necessary, but first he must find the lost one and try to pick up the track of the killer dog.

Jet still sat guarding the dead sheep: seven now, for the life had gone out of the other two. She bristled in every hair and growled in the back of her throat as she looked round her in the dusk.

Matthew threw the dead sheep into the Landrover: they were heavy and awkward and he sweated with the effort. Then he looked about him. There seemed no clue to where the dog had gone, but Jet seemed convinced he was about somewhere and she cast eagerly back and forth, trying to puzzle out his scent among that of the sheep.

The dog knew she was there as he lay upwind of her, crouched in a ditch. He had seen the man approaching with a gun on his shoulder and had dropped out of sight. Above him on the bank lay the dead lamb. He wanted to eat it, but he had not dared stir while there were such comings and goings of the man and his vehicle. He was growing hungry now though, for he had spent a good while chasing and killing, without stopping to satisfy his appetite. The chase had been enough—the excitement of the blundering bodies and the warmth of wool and blood—but now he needed to eat. When the man had gone he would take the lamb and gorge himself.

Matthew walked about the field in the deceptive grey light. Every small bush could have been a lamb or a crouched dog. His eyes ached with looking. Then at last he saw the dead lamb on the bank, ran towards it and stooped down, setting the gun beside him.

The grey dog looked up and saw the man crouched over the kill and he saw that the gun was not in his hand. Then he rose up out of the ditch in the dusk and challenged Matthew with a choking snarl. He had been well trained to his job and he was not afraid to attack. His only fear was the gun.

There was no time between the moment Matthew became aware of the dog and the moment of attack. The Alsatian launched himself and Matthew stood no chance of avoiding him, but in spite of his utter surprise and amazement that a dog should attack in this way, he managed to lunge sideways so that the jaws took him by the shoulder rather than the throat. The dog's teeth pierced the heavy cloth of his jacket and burned into the muscle of Matthew's upper arm, so that he staggered and almost went down. He tried to twist to get a hold on the grey fur, and he knew in himself the panic that the sheep must have felt. He was convinced the dog meant to kill him.

Then suddenly, and to Matthew's immense relief, the fierce hold was released, and dazed and shocked as he was, Matthew was quick to see the reason. Clinging like a leech to the grey dog was the slight black shape of Jet. She had him by the ear and her teeth had met through it. She would not let go, though the Alsatian lunged and swung violently, trying to rid himself of the pain.

The collie's usual fighting method is the slashing bite and the quick retreat, but Jet hung on: she would not give this dog a chance to attack her master again. The grey body and the black body rolled together like a dust storm and a terrible muffled noise of savagery rose from them.

Matthew had the shotgun in his hands now and stood by, helplessly, waiting for the chance to use it. There was blood all over Jet as the grey dog bit her whenever he could lay jaws to her, but she would not let go. Then, trying a new tactic, the Alsatian braced his legs and flung his head and neck round, like a bull set upon by a terrier, until he worked up enough force to dash Jet to the ground so heavily that the breath was knocked out of her and she lost her hold.

The grey dog's ear was spurting blood and he turned on Jet in fury, determined to finish her and free now to get a grip where he would, but Matthew had the gun on him and the bullet smashed into him at close range. The Alsatian's jaws had opened as if to take Jet by the throat, but they slackened then, the blood poured out of them, and he fell dead.

Till that moment Matthew had been aware of the dog first as a menacing shadow and then as a terrible adversary, but looking down at its shattered body, he recognized what dog it was and was glad he had made an end of it.

He turned from it and stooped over

Jet, who lay quite still on the ground, her sense overwhelmed by the ferocity of the fight and the close-hand blast of the shotgun. He ran his hands over her and they came away red. He could feel no broken bones, though, so he picked her up and carried her to the car, stumbling as he went and cursing the world with every foul word in his memory. His tears fell on her black fur, but they did not rouse her.

'Don't knock so loud. The world's not due to end yet.' George Aiken, the vet, walked down the long passage to his door, wishing that people would not encourage their animals to have accidents, diseases, difficult births and sudden deaths the moment he had settled down for the night. Here was another one, bang, bang, bang, and him only just out of his bath. He opened the door.

'My God,' he said when he saw Matthew there on the step with Jet in his arms. 'What war have you two been fighting?'

He bustled them both into the surgery,

prised Jet away from Matthew, whose grip seemed so fixed upon her that his muscles were unwilling to let go, and laid the injured collie on the table. He then went into the dispensary and came back with several items of equipment on a tray, and also a small bowl of antiseptic and a glass of whisky. He pushed Matthew down into a chair and set the last two items down beside him.

'That's to clean up your shoulder,' he said, indicating the bowl, 'and the good stuff's for your gut. Down it quick, man, and then attend to yourself while I see to the dog.'

Aiken switched on the bright light over the surgery table and examined Jet very carefully. Then he began to work on her: giving injections, cleaning, stitching, totally absorbed. Matthew watched, thankful that under the caked blood and fur the tears in Jet's flesh, though long and wicked enough, were not so bad as he had feared, and her breathing was steady and strong, though she had not yet come to her senses, and would not for a while, drugged now against pain by Aiken's needle.

They were lucky to have a vet like him. He was a short, square man, strong as a blacksmith, but when the village kids brought injured birds to him, doomed though most of the rescued bundles of feathers were by their hearts' reaction to the intensity of their fear, he would cradle them softly in his great ham hands and speak words of comfort to their rescuers.

What was wrong with Jet was for the most part self-evident, but Matthew knew from past experience Aiken's skill in diagnosing condition and disease in his speechless, often uncooperative, frequently plain bad-tempered patients. Where other vets seemed to find out the trouble by process of eliminating what it was *not,* Aiken had a genius for seeing almost at once what it was. He was murmuring to himself now, as he worked, recording the extent of each wound in his mind as he dressed it. He would be aware exactly of the progress of its healing when next he examined it.

When he had finished, and Jet lay there quietly, clean and stitched, George Aiken turned to Matthew and said, 'You should see a doctor.'

'Later,' Matthew said. 'You see to me, will you?'

'You'll get me struck off,' the vet said. 'I'll look at that shoulder, but you must see Sands in the morning. Now tell me what happened.'

Matthew had made a start on cleaning up the jagged bite on his shoulder, but while Aiken continued the job he explained what had taken place and how he had killed the grey Alsatian.

'Well, thank the Lord you did,' the vet commented. 'Now you ought to have an anti-tet for that bite, and you be thankful we've no rabies here yet.'

'I've had all the jabs,' Matthew said, 'I'm not a fool.'

'When?'

'After the fire. The full course. Started in hospital and I had the final one last September.

'Well, you'll do then, but Sands may want to stitch this and give you a booster. Mind you see him.'

'OK.'

Both men stood by the table and watched Jet, waiting for her to come round. Matthew stationed himself where she would see him at once when she woke. At last her eyes opened and her tail quivered at the sight of him.

'That's good,' Aiken said.

'Shall I take her home?' Matthew was eager, delighted that she was conscious again.

'Not on your life,' the vet said. 'There are a good many tests I want to do before I let her out of my sight. I know you shepherds. You'll have her galloping up and down hill in a brace of shakes and splitting all my nice, expensive stitches.' He grinned at Matthew and put a hand on his shoulder. 'Go home now, there's a good fellow. I'll bring her over the moment she's fit, and she'll be far too dozy to pine for you for a day or so.'

Matthew acknowledged the good sense

of what Aiken said despite his teasing manner of saying it. He laid a hand briefly on Jet's head and said, 'Stay there quiet, little bitch. Nobody's indispensable, you know.'

He walked out of the surgery very quickly and stood in the cold air of very early morning to collect himself. Then he got into the Landrover. There was blood all over the front seats and in the back the dead sheep lolled, smelling of muck and blood and greasy wool. There had been no time to chuck them out.

'God, what a mess,' said Matthew to himself. He opened all the windows and drove towards home in the early light. He would send a message to the Hunt Kennels. His disaster would be a windfall for them. 'And a dead loss to me,' he shouted at a startled hare that browsed by the roadside. It leaped away, affronted, into a field of growing corn and sat at a safe distance, erect, like a miniature kangaroo, nibbling the green heads of the wheat. The birds were beginning to sing the dawn in, but

Matthew was in no mood to listen.

He arrived at Flint Hill and threw the dead sheep in the old lean-to shed where he stored odd bits of machinery. The sheep were in no position to object to their housing.

He went then and tended the injured ones in the stable. They should have been seen to long since, but he had left everything to rush Jet to Aiken's. He was lucky though: the injuries were slight. They had been more frightened than hurt and had now recovered their composure. He dressed their cuts with iodine and threw them some hay. Then he fed the rest of the flock in the bull-pen, for they were hungry, having quickly demolished the few tufts of weedy grass that grew there. He would check them over later, then let them out into the Home Field. Ewes and lambs could run together a while longer. They had had shocks enough, without adding to them.

He milked the cows; he milked Bella and staked her out on the bank; he fed the chickens, and then he went in for his breakfast. The house was very still.

Then her remembered his promise, and having cleaned the inside of the Landrover so that it no longer resembled a slaughter-house, he put on a clean shirt and drove down to see Dr Sands. It was not surgery time, but Sands would always see farming men at odd hours, considering their time to be almost as precious as his own.

Sands was a young man—or at least, the village thought him so. He had taken over from Dr Cokes, who had been part of the ordering of life and death in Shepley and the surrounding hamlets and farm-steads for many, many years. The new doctor had been five years in Shepley now and was finally becoming accepted, though at the beginning his straight talk and his blunt refusal to pander to his patients' whims had caused mutterings amounting almost to mutiny in the ranks, and there were one or two who still preferred the long ride to Clipton to see Dr Varley. Sands was a country man though and not afraid of a bit of mud when visiting on his rounds, so the farming community approved of him.

He was very much surprised though when Matthew came in to see him, but he greeted him cheerfully and asked what was up. He had hardly set eyes on the man since he had left hospital. Matthew explained about the attack the sheep-worrier had made on him and Sands examined the shoulder.

'So Aiken cleaned that up for you, did he? Nice job he made of it too. Wish I'd make as good a vet as he'd make a doctor. It'd be nice to have patients that don't answer back, too. I'd like that.'

'I remember that Groves' old stallion used to argue a fair bit,' said Matthew.

'Right you are. I'll stick to my last,' said the doctor. 'I'm going to put a stitch or two in that, just to finish off a good job. All right?'

'All right,' said Matthew.

While that was going on, Sands looked carefully at his patient. Could they have tried hard enough at the hospital to persuade Ratton to have some cosmetic work done on those scars? Probably they had. Obstinate chap at the best of times. Fine shepherd though. Good farmer all round.

'Are they going to see you again at the General?' he asked.

'What for?' Matthew inquired.

'Do a bit of patchwork on that face. They can—'

' "Do wonders these days",' Matthew cut in. 'I just want to be left well alone.'

'It's your face,' said Sands.

'Right,' said Matthew and the doctor went quietly on with his work.

The conversation reminded Matthew of Mary West. What exotic place was she gadding around in? Peggy Davey seemed to like the girl well enough and more than once had tried to talk to Matthew about her, but he thought he'd made it clear now that he didn't want to know. He had no time for women like that.

CHAPTER 12

He put up with it for two days: the lone-
liness in the house; the temptation to go
out just once more to look down the
track for Aiken's car. What a fool he was
to care so much for a dog. She was just a
dog. She would have her fourteen years
or so, with luck, but that would be the
end of it. For all that, he was content to
be a fool.

The second evening he walked down
to the Dog and Partridge. He did not
really want company, but neither did he
wish to be alone, so he found a seat in the
corner, with his good side turned to the
world so that he should cause no
comment, sympathetic or otherwise. He
thought he would like to get drunk,
slowly, so as to pass the time. He had two
drinks and watched the people come and
go. It seemed to be a busy night. Jimmy

Peel smiled across at him from behind the bar but he was too busy to come over and talk. Matthew was glad. Then a familiar voice spoke in his ear, 'Matthew. What are you doing here?'

It was Patty. He had not seen her since the painful hour when she had come to visit him in hospital. She had tried to talk to him without looking at him and he had found nothing to say at all. Twice since then he had heard she was to be married, but there was no ring on her finger now. Spoiled for choice and couldn't make up her mind, he supposed. He cast his mind back to the old days, before she had gone to Bristol. Patty of the inviting eyes, the luscious body, the accommodating morals. Was that in his lifetime or in someone else's? She'd be, how many years older now? There wasn't much difference in the look of her, except that she was, if it were possible, a little more buxom across the front where the breasts were constrained by her sweater as she leaned over him, assuming a welcome, sure of her effect.

She pulled up a chair and sat by him, though she had been given no invitation. She peered into his almost empty glass and called across to a group of people at the far end of the bar, for a refill for Matthew and a gin and tonic for herself.

With another drink inside him he felt able to talk to her. Small-talk, though, as if they hardly knew each other, which was true he supposed. He bought her a drink in his turn and yet another for himself, and he looked hard at the attractions of Patty James and decided with relief that he had grown out of her. Strangely, that made it easier to talk to her and with the next drink he began to feel quite relaxed, leaning across to take her hand, to see what her reaction would be. She did not seem to object and talked animatedly to him, leaving her hand in his.

Her friends at the bar drifted over, and there was another round of drinks. Matthew was persuaded to chase the beer he had been drinking with whisky.

Not long after that it became necessary

for him to go to the lavatory. His legs seemed to have uncoordinated springs where the knee-joints should be.

When he got back, Patty and her friends were all standing at the bar.

'What a wreck,' one of the men was saying. 'Can't think why you bother, Patty.'

'Oh, come on,' another girl said. 'You have to be kind, don't you?'

'Let's go on into Clipton,' Patty said. 'It's a dead and alive hole, this. Old fashioned as hell. Let's go to the King's Head. They'll have music there.'

The group went out, noisily, not noticing Matthew standing by the inner door. He walked to the bar.

'I'll have another drink, Jimmy.'

Jimmy was curious to discover what Matthew Ratton was doing here without his dog, knowing he would as soon be about without his right arm, but the expression on the farmer's face did not encourage questions. He had had more than enough to drink too, and that was sure.

'You've had a fair amount, Matthew,' he said.

What's that to you? I want to drink a toast. To hell with all women.'

It grew very warm in the Dog and Partridge and the wafting smoke in the atmosphere made Matthew's eyes sting. It would be better to be outside. He wished John Davey had been in tonight. They could have talked. Oh well, perhaps better not. He would go outside now and sit for a while and then he would walk back to Flint Hill. Or he could go to Pennant. No, maybe not. Peggy would give him what for. And he would have to tell them about Jet. He didn't want to talk about Jet.

He walked out of the door into the dark, glad to clear his head in the cool, large air of the night. An immeasurable distance above him, the stars moved in their slow courses. They seemed to him to wheel and dance. How beautiful they were, these remote companions of his nocturnal watches. He did not need people when his life embraced the stars and the whole landscape in which he had his being. What was it the poet said? It haunted him like a passion. He would not bother any more with people. People were rubbish. He would watch the cloud shapes on the hills, and feel the wind driving through the trees as if they were stalks of wheat, and walk the hilltops alone, and that would be enough for him. So damn people. People could rot for all he cared.

It seemed a long way to Flint Hill and the walk up to the house seemed steeper than usual. Added to that, the ditches on either hand moved disconcertingly towards him if he did not concentrate very hard on where to place his feet. He sang a little, to keep his spirits up. It was not generally appreciated how well he could sing. Beautiful if was. He sang again. 'The spacious firmament on high.' It seemed to him that perhaps he had not quite got all the words right, but it was very lovely, for all that.

When he woke in the morning with his head on the kitchen table at Flint Hill and his arms dangling uncomfortably down, he could not clearly remember how he had got there. His mouth felt as if it were full of floor-sweepings and his eyes objected to the light. It was very bright light. For the first time ever he was late milking and when he went down to the gate, grey and shaky and generally wretched, the cows lowed mournfully at him, reproaching his neglect.

He moved about in the cowhouse as awkwardly as a man in space and every noise of the machinery vibrated in his head like the clangour of bells. 'It serves you right,' he said to himself. 'It serves you bloody well right.'

At last the cows were all emptied and ready to go back to pasture again. The big cooling tank frothed with white milk. The floor of the parlour was hosed and gleaming.

Matthew led Bella to where her stake and chain awaited her. She was full of capricious fun, in spite of her mature years, and he felt that if she tugged away from him like that just once again his head would likely fall right off, but he got her safely fastened at last.

It was then that he heard the sound of an engine and he turned round to see George Aiken's old Morris come up the hill towards the yard. He went to meet it, feeling absurdly excited. The vet got out. He looked very hard at Matthew but made no comment. Then he opened the back door of the car and out came Jet— very stiff and slow and lame in her near hind leg, but on her feet and under her own steam. She hobbled towards Matthew and he crouched down to her and seized her by the long ruff-hairs behind her ears. He could not speak to her, but just held her and looked. George Aiken went over to Bella and engaged her in a conversation of some length.

At last Matthew said, 'She'll be all right now, will she?' and Aiken came over, smiling, to assure him the bitch would be fine, though she would limp for a while yet.

'So if you're satisfied, I'll be off now, Matthew. The West girl's horse is lame and she wants him looked at.'

Matthew made a dismissive noise.

'It seems she lent him to a friend while she was away and he put a hind foot in a rabbit hole. It'll be no more than a sprain, I dare say.'

'And what sunny spot has she been off to this time?'

'Kandara,' said the vet and he gave Matthew a curious look. That was an odd place to choose, Matthew thought. There had been civil war in Kandara, and riots in the aftermath, and if that were not enough, there had been a recent series of minor earthquakes. Still, there was no accounting for taste.

'There's one thing,' Matthew said. 'She'll have no problem paying your bill if she can afford holidays like that.'

George Aiken stared at Matthew with raised eyebrows. 'Holidays?' he said. 'What on earth are you talking about?' She's not there on holiday. She's been working in the refugee transit camps. She's a trained nurse. Surely you knew that?'

Matthew shook his head, very slowly, as if it were full of rocks.

'You don't mean to tell me that just because she's attractive and looks good on a fine horse, you thought she was some kind of flighty deb, or a "jet setter" or whatever they call the bright young things these days? Man, what an idiot you are!'

Aiken began to laugh and he laughed a good deal, until he caught a look in Matthew's eye that warned him to stop.

'She calved my heifer for me,' Matthew said.

'I'm not surprised. She'd tackle anything,' said the vet. 'Now look, I must be off. Get that dog indoors, and don't work her for at least a week.'

'All right,' said Matthew.

He took Jet into the kitchen and settled her in her bed. She was still very weak and her coat was marred where the hair had been cut back from the gashes the grey dog had given her. She lapped some warm milk that Matthew brought her and looked up at him gratefully. Now she was back with him and in her familiar place, she was content. She sighed happily and put her head on her paws. He sat with his chair tilted back upon its hinder legs as he often did, with his boots on the corner of the table. His hand and arm trailed down beside him, stirring every now and again to scratch her ears. She breathed in the reassuring smell of him, after the strange, aseptic cleanliness of the surgery that had made her so uneasy, and listened to the flow of his voice. He spoke to her at length, telling her things she did not understand, and sometimes she sensed sadness and anger in him, but she knew that they were none of her causing, for the fingers continued to caress her head and ears. Soon she fell asleep.

When he saw that she was sleeping, Matthew grinned wryly. 'So I can't even keep *you* awake with my troubles, little bitch. I'll leave you in peace and get on with the work.'

He went out to look at the sheep. They were grazing contentedly, with no memory of past horrors. One or two glanced up, recognized him and bleated, then fell to grazing again. When feed was short and he arrived with sacks of grass-nuts and flaked maize for them, they all came pouring towards him in a woolly flood; shoving, butting, imperative. This was the fat time of the year, though, and there was enough good grass for all.

The cows looked well on it, with sleek, shining hides. They were hippy, of course, not padded all over like John Davey's beeves, for they gave their all to the milk and their yields were hearteningly good. Matthew walked down and watched them too, as they wrapped their tongues about the long stalks in the rich pasture, and swallowed the green-stuff down into the intricate, many-stomached mysteries of their innards. Sal, the horned one, belched loudly and began to chew her cud as she stood in the shade under a tree. There in the shadow the flies did not pester so much. There were warble-flies about, but the cows were all dressed against them. If warbles struck the cattle, their backs eventually became covered in unsightly lumps the size of walnuts, each containing a revolting fat maggot that must be squeezed out and destroyed. It was a job Matthew had been given as a boy, and he could remember very clearly the bucketsful of those disgusting objects that he had removed from some half-dozen stricken members of the herd, and how in their irritation his patients had swung their heads at him and stood upon his feet and swiped at him with their tails.

He went on down to the hayfields. The weather looked like settling. The cutter blades on the mowing machine were sharp and set ready. He would make a start before long. He could hear, further down the valley, the rattle and clank of machinery on Pennant Farm, for John Davey always started early on his hay, to get it clear before corn harvest. It would be an idea to walk down to see if he needed a hand to get the bales in, and perhaps tell him about Jet, now the crisis was over. He felt in the mood for a good long talk with John Davey. Maybe there were some people worth talking to.

CHAPTER 13

Each day Jet grew a little stronger, and took greater exception to being left behind in the kitchen when Matthew went out. She had been visited by Peggy Davey and treated like royalty. Aiken had been back to see her and to report that she was doing splendidly, but she pined to be out and about with Matthew again, doing the job she was trained for. He hated to see her so chafed by the enforced restraint and on a day of brilliant sunshine, when the work had gone well and the hayfields were all shorn but not yet ready for baling, he decided to spare an hour to take her out in the car, just for the ride. She would enjoy that.

They drove up to the hilltop near Brierley. There would be a breeze there. It was even hotter than Matthew had realized and the valley was too still. What an odd climate it was, to be sure, that could make you winter-cold and then bring you out in a muck-sweat within a handful of days. Matthew had known years when there had been frost in June that had seared all the young green off the beech trees and then again he had known it so hot at the end of April that he could work in the fields stripped to the waist. Today would be a scorcher, no doubt about that.

They got out of the Landrover and walked across the turf for a hundred yards or so, going slowly for Jet's sake, and Matthew sat down on a rock at the point where the hill dropped steeply away to the valley. There were butter-flies flitting idly about and bees in the yellow gorseflowers and larks that had risen up from the lower meadows, hover-ing on a level with his eyes, nearly bursting themselves with singing.

Matthew gazed about him at all this and at the tumbled rocks and vivid bracken. Once they had planned to drive a road through here. Granted, there was a road already—narrow, unobtrusive and useful to the neighbourhood—but there had been great plans in high places to widen and lengthen it and fuse it with the road that went into Clipton, so that through-traffic could bypass the town and people could get to somewhere else just that little bit faster. It would have taken a great bite out of the Pennant land, too, and brought with it all the hazards that a fast road and too many people always bring to a farmer's livelihood. Yet it had not been the possible invasion of John Davey's workshop that had reversed the decision but the pressure brought to bear by the conservationists, who feared for the wildlife on Brierly Hill where there were orchises and some butterfly species scarcely found anywhere else. Matthew knew of these, of course, and had been anxious for them too. They had not been rarities when his mother was alive and there were drawings of them in plenty in her notebooks. She had loved them for their beauty, not realizing that they might one day be almost extinguished by progress. Matthew was glad they were safe, but it seemed an odd and perplexing world where a working man's needs stood for less than the needs of a butterfly.

He watched the larks again, their voices shaking their small bodies as they soared until they vanished in the dazzle of the sun.

'And what are they singing about, do you think, my Jet?' he asked her. 'Not, "Look at me, I'm beautiful and it's a glorious day and I can sing like an angel from heaven." That's not it, my little lass. "Push off," they're saying, each to the other. "Push off you lot, this is my patch." You have to be practical, my girl. There's no two ways about it. But I'm glad they left this place for the butterflies, for all that.'

Matthew got up and stretched himself and they walked on a little further, Jet enjoying the breeze in her ears and the soft turf under her pads. Here and there were small bunches of sheep, the Tally Cottage sheep, and these she looked over with a professional eye. Then, as she and Matthew were passing a great tangled clump of briars, she stopped and barked. Matthew called her but she remained where she was and barked again.

Trapped in the briars, with long bramble stems firmly embedded in her fleece, was a sheep. Each long pliable stalk was bound around with strands of wool, holding her fast, and she stood panting, too exhausted to bleat. Matthew took out his horn-handled knife and carefully cut her free. It took him several minutes and all the while she stood and trembled, with hanging head. And while he worked, Matthew was increasingly aware of the disgusting smell that came from her. She was fly-struck. Once she was free, he could see the maggots heave and writhe on the raw flesh where the fleece had peeled away. The foul creatures were literally eating her alive. Matthew turned his head away and spat, to relieve his feelings.

So much for Mary West then. So she was a nurse, was she? So he had been mistaken. Maybe so, but he was not wrong about her altogether, was he, if she'd let an animal of hers get into this state, and suffer as this ewe was suffering? If that girl was at home, then the sooner she saw the results of her neglect, the better.

He and Jet between them eased the ewe gently along to the car and bundled her inside. Matthew had knocked the maggots from her back and ground them satisfyingly under his heel. He had some old-fashioned Green-Oils Ointment in the front compartment and this he used to give immediate relief to her sores, but she would need further treatment as soon as possible.

In the garden of Tally Cottage, Mary West stood waist-high in weeds, wielding a swap-hook whose edge seemed to blunt at every stroke, for the nettles and hogweed and fools' parsley had run rampant. She'd get a pig in here, that would be best. Too much like hard work otherwise. She ran the whetstone once more along the curved blade and took a huge, swiping blow at a clump of bed-straw. The tip of the hook bounced off a stone and nicked her shin. It was not much of a cut but it hurt and she sat down to clasp a broad leaf over it to ease the stinging. She had done as much for the children in the camps when they were short of dressings. She had soon learned which leaves were the most effective.

She was sitting there with the tall grasses towering over her when Matthew arrived in the Landrover. She had not expected to see him, even though George Aiken had told her about the strange misconception the farmer had had about her. Why had Matthew come to see her, and of all things, brought her a sheep? She was not going to make things easy for him by being too welcoming. She rose to meet him, taking him off his guard. He had thought the garden was empty. She looked at him, unsmiling.

' *"Et dona ferentes,"* ' she said.

'This is hardly a gift,' he snapped at her. All the dramatic and accusatory sentences he had composed to launch at her when they met seemed to have deserted him.

She looked carefully at the sheep. 'What a mess,' she said.

'It's one of yours,' said Matthew. 'I found her on the hill.' He looked for traces of shame in her expression, but saw nothing but sudden anger.

'Now look,' she said, bristling at him, 'I paid Fielding good money to stay on as shepherd until I'd disposed of the lease. I'd wanted to ask you if you'd do it. Remember the day the heifer calved? Well, that was why I came up to Flint Hill, to ask if you'd consider shepherding for me, but with the way things turned out, I asked Fielding instead. I knew I wouldn't have time to care for the flock and he assured me he'd see to them. Good Heavens, you didn't think I'd deliberately let them rot, did you?'

Now it came to it, he didn't. It wasn't in character, even in his original warped version of her character. 'Well,' he said uncomfortably aware that he should apologize and quite unable to do so,

'Fielding's a rotten shepherd and always was.' He paused, feeling awkward, and then said suddenly, on a rush of breath, 'Let me have the lease. I've waited a long while for it. Then there'll be no worries about the sheep for you or for me.'

She looked at him.

'I'll pay the going rate,' he said and for a moment or so she continued to regard him with an expression he could not quite fathom.

Then, 'I suppose that would be the practical solution,' she agreed.

She held her hand out to seal the agreement. Her arm was slender and brown and covered in bramble scratches. Her grass-stained shirt was open at the neck and her skin smelt of sunshine and mint-leaves from the tangled garden. Urgently, overwhelmingly, he wanted her, and he felt again that sudden coursing in the blood that had taken him so much by surprise before. What was he to do? Even if he wished to make his feelings known, she was hardly likely to think much of him now, the way he had behaved. Best go home, put her out of his mind. Settle the lease by letter. Keep it all businesslike.

He bent to pick up the sheep. 'I'd best take her home,' he said. 'She needs attention.'

'All right,' she replied and smiled. 'I'm glad your dog's so fit again by the way. George told me about the Alsatian. It sounded like a really nasty experience for you and Jet.'

'I wouldn't want it again,' said Matthew. 'But it could have been worse. You have to take George Aiken's tales with a pinch of salt, you know.'

'Do I?' she said.

He roared up the track from Tally Cottage, using his gears as if the Landrover were a racing car, and the protesting machinery seemed to relieve his confused and confusing emotions. He was out of the habit of feeling anything at all for other people, except perhaps the filial affection he felt for the Daveys. Yet, in spite of himself, it seemed, if he got too close to Mary West he felt knocked sideways by her. It was ridiculous.

He drove home rather too quickly and tried to stop thinking about her. He attended to the ewe he had brought back from the hill and made her comfortable in the stable. She bleated for a while for her distant companions, then gave up and lay wearily in the straw, at ease now and rid of the intolerable itching that had plagued her so long. He'd tell Fielding where she was, but he doubted the man would care much, though he'd be damned angry to know Matthew had got the lease.

Jet was weary too, after her outing, and limped to her accustomed place on the rug to stretch herself out and doze for a while. Matthew fidgeted about the room, restless, arranging and rearranging objects whose places had been unchanged for a year or more.

Well, he had the lease, so that was something. There was nothing in writing, but they had shaken on the deal and that was good enough. He remembered again that handshake and looked down at his own stained hand, half expecting it to show the imprint of her palm on his and the marks of her fingers on the back, so vividly did he recall their pressure.

CHAPTER 14

The bales were in and filled the barn with their sweetness. They were a pleasure to all the senses: to the eye for their plenty, and the subtle, faded green of them; to the nostrils; and to the touch and the hearing, for the rustling dryness of them showed they were of well-saved hay that would not moulder, or worse still, catch fire by slow combustion. Above all, they were a pleasure in that they represented good food for the hungry months, when the grass would rest and lose its nourishment and the beasts would come to the gates each day expecting to be provided for.

Matthew was whistling cheerfully then, as he walked down to Pennant with Jet, to collect the post and compare crops with John Davey, and maybe stay and talk for a while. As he approached the first Pennant gate he saw his old friend hurrying down the track towards him, and was taken completely aback when John Davey shouted, 'Stop! Stop where you are. Don't come any nearer!'

'What on earth is wrong?' Matthew called back.

'For God's sake, Matthew, stay there. I'll come as close as I dare.'

John Davey looked ash-grey and more worried than Matthew could ever remember seeing him. His shoulders sagged as if a heavy weight were on him. He stopped some twenty yards from the gate and called out, 'Aiken's just been to see one of my beeves. It was going unsound this morning. He says there's a chance it might be foot-and-mouth.'

'Oh God!' said Matthew. 'Which beast is it?'

'One of that half dozen I had off Harry Stevens a week back.'

Well, that was a good turn gone bad if ever there was one. Harry Stevens was an old chap going on eighty who had kept a smallholding down the valley from

Pennant: a dreadful place, all docks and corrugated iron and never a gate but was tied up with baler twine in three or four places.

Harry had gone off to an old people's home and John Davey had bought up his few head of stock at the auction because the bidding was slow and he did not want to see the old man lose out on the beasts. He would have kept the creatures away from his own, of course, being a prudent man, but that would be no safeguard if one of them was really infected with foot-and-mouth.

It was the terror of their lives, that disease. It had first struck the country a century and a half ago, and there was little more that could be done about it now than there was then. When it struck, the affected farm would be isolated and all but the most essential visitors forbidden. There would be antiseptic washes at the entrance gates, through which every wheel and boot must pass. Other farms, as yet uninfected, would take this precaution too and would often try other preventative measures that were more akin to witchcraft than medicine, such as rubbing the doorposts of the stables and barns with garlic or onions. No one knew for sure how the disease spread, in the swift and sometimes apparently inconsequential way that it did, and many blamed foxes, or rats or even birds, so that there was often panicky slaughter of every whisker and feather of wildlife that showed itself on the farms. The result for an infected farm was always the same though. Every cloven-hoofed beast must be killed and burned and the once busy yards and well-stocked fields would be empty and desolate. Provident men were insured, of course, but good farmers had regard for their beasts, more than as mere living investments of their capital. They knew their natures, their characters and their breeding, and were, for the most part, fond of them. When the time came to put an end to their stay at the farm, whether by way of the market or the butcher, they were not sentimental about it, because that was the way of things, but the abrupt destruction and wastage of prime beasts was enough to break a man's spirit.

'You'd best go round by the long track, Matthew, when you go into Shepley,' John said. 'There was no post for you today anyway and I've told Posty to leave ours in the old pheasantry but down below, so you'd best look for yours there too. Just for a day or so, you know. Till we're sure, one way or the other.'

'Ok, John,' Matthew said. There was nothing he could do for John Davey that would be more useful than keeping away. He began to walk slowly back to Flint Hill and raised a hand in salute to the older man standing alone in the middle of the stony track.

Matthew thought about him all that day, and Peggy too. What must she feel about the possible slaughter of all their beasts? Well, if George Aiken brought back the unwelcome verdict, they would all of them stand in danger of infection, all the farms in the area, Flint Hill among them, despite John Davey's immediate and stringent precautions. Notices would be posted, footpaths closed, markets cancelled, transport of animals forbidden.

The day went slow and hung heavy, and Matthew felt quite unable to settle to any of the minor jobs about the farm that awaited him. A gloomy demon in his mind kept suggesting that it could all be a waste of time, that everything might be reduced to ashes just as surely as by the fire, and that there might be no beasts left to eat the good hay in the barn.

There was a blustering wind that night that took a day or so to blow itself out and some mornings later he saw a sizeable branch from one of the beeches had fallen onto the barn roof. It was still attached to the tree by a few sinews of wood and as the tree moved, the branch moved, scraping and scratching over the paintwork, and pulling at the bolts that held down the corrugated iron. He would need to cut that away before it did further damage. Because it was a job outside routine he was somehow able to shake off his persistent gloom and put his mind to it. The barn was set against the bank, so that it was possible to climb to the roof quite easily with the help of a ladder, and from the roof to climb onto one of the sound branches of the tree in order to cut off the damaged one. Once sawn through, it would probably slide to the ground under its own weight.

He got himself braced safely in the tree. He had no fear of heights, but had a great respect for them, for all that. Then he cut through the grey skin of the beech-bark and into the creamy wood beneath, to remove the damaged branch close up to the trunk and not leave an unsightly spiked end behind. He had finished the job to his satisfaction and had watched the branch slither to the ground when he became aware of movement in the fields away to his right. A party of hikers had left the right-of-way that skirted his boundary in that direction and were taking a short cut across his field. There must have been twenty of them, in shorts and shirts or anoraks, with bright-coloured frame rucksacks and bundles of tents and pots and pans enough for an army cookhouse. He could hear the faint clangour of these as the wind brought the sound of their passing towards him along the valley. One after the other the hikers climbed his boundary wall and strode off across the field, where the ewes were grazing. They opened the far gate and went through and he saw the last two look at each other as if to say, 'Your turn to shut the gate, old chap'. And neither of them did.

Matthew bellowed between cupped hands, 'Shut the bloody gate, can't you?' But the wind was against him and they did not hear. One of the ewes raised her head from the grass and began to trot towards the opening. One by one, the others began to follow. Grey woollen shapes streamed over the grass, moving purposefully to the gateway, to the track that led downhill and eventually to Pennant, and not even the ungrazed sward on either side would tempt them to stop if the whim took them to move on downward.

Matthew yelled for Jet who lay at the ladder's foot. At his command she went off after them, but she was still lame and slow. By the time he had descended the ladder she was at the far side of the field by the open gateway, but the sheep were well ahead of her. Matthew ran, cursing at every breath, choking on his own sense of panic. There seemed to be a great pressure in his head which was more than the effect of a pounding heart and stretched lungs. If he could have laid hands on any one of those hikers at that moment he would have throttled the life out of him and been glad to do it. Then, as he too reached the open gateway and looked down the long track that stretched away down the slope, he saw the flock in the distance approaching a further gateway, with Jet almost at their heels but not yet quite able to reach them. Then he saw a horse and rider approaching, from the Pennant side of the gate: saw the rider make more speed at the sight of the sheep and deftly slam the further gate in their faces as they raced towards it. It was Mary West, of course. Well, she'd turned his sheep for him, but what in God's name was she doing riding through Pennant land? Didn't she know about foot-and-mouth? Hadn't John Davey put up notices enough? He ran towards her, starved of breath and sour in his stomach with an indigestible mixture of relief and anger.

'What the hell are you doing?' he shouted.

'Turning your sheep,' she said. 'I assume you wanted them stopped?'

He glowered at her and muttered something half-audible about supposing he ought to be grateful, but she should keep clear of Pennant land while the scare was on.

'Damn it, you seem determined to make me grateful to you, one way or another,' he said, like a surly child.

She looked at him, hard and proud as diamond, and said in a voice of as crystal a quality, 'Gratitude's the last thing I want from you, Matthew Ratton. If I'd let your sheep run on to Pennant you would have suffered no more than a longer chase for your pains. John Davey asked me to come up and tell you his farm is clear and there's no danger. The lame beast had foul-of-the-foot from being in that dirty barn of Mr Stevens' and the mouth ulcers were caused by eating bits of rubbish in with its hay. So you see I could have carried no disease onto your land and I'll carry none away except disgust at your ill manners.'

She wheeled the bay horse and set him off at a smart canter down the track, leaving Matthew staring after her with open mouth. For a long time he watched her, until the distance claimed her. It occurred to him then that he felt for the first time in many years reproved and chastened, and not resentful.

'Served you bloody right, that did,' he said, and ran a finger reflectively down his face. It was the second time in a short while this unwilling conclusion had been dragged from him.

He turned to Jet who lay panting at the side of the track, holding the sheep penned against the closed gate.

'Jet,' he said. 'Did you hear me? It served me bloody well right.' And he laughed and laughed till the tears flowed down his face and a brace of pigeons came clattering out of the trees in amazement with a noise like desultory applause.

'Well, what are you waiting for?' he said to Jet. 'You're not crippled yet. Let's get the sheep home.'

The little bitch looked at him under her brows, not sure how to react to his sudden outburst of laughter, but he seemed himself again now, quite sane and reasonable, so she made her usual half-circle to gather the sheep and get them moving homeward, and even allowed herself one exasperated bark at the old full-mouthed ewe that had set them off on their travels and who felt that she would like to keep her freedom a little longer.

Down on the main road the hikers

waited for the bus to take them back to town.

'That was great,' said one. 'The air up there does you a power of good, I reckon. I wouldn't mind living up there.'

'Fancy being a farmer, do you?' another asked.

'Yeah,' he replied. 'Reckon I could make a go of it.'

At Pennant, John Davey watched the beef cattle ambling across to the trough and quenching their thirst with long satisfying pulls at the water. He watched them with conscious pleasure, as one might look at a treasured object that has been misplaced and at long last found again. There was a great deal waiting to be done, but for a while he would stand and consider how good it was that it remained for the doing.

CHAPTER 15

In the next days Matthew watched out for the bay horse on the hill, half expecting to see him breast the skyline where the bridle track came down from Brierley or to hear the muffled beat of his hooves on the sheep turf in the waltz-time rhythm of his easy, loping canter. The landscape remained empty though of all but its usual wildlife and the sheep dotted here and there, grazing or moving as the fancy took them. The horse was not to be seen in his paddock next to the Dog and Partridge either, and Tally Cottage was shut fast, with none of the familiar clutter about it that may be expected of an occupied dwelling; boots at the doorsill, a saucer where some animal has fed, a bucket waiting to be taken somewhere. It was neat and swept and empty.

'Ridden over to her cousin's at Holton I shouldn't wonder,' was Jimmy Peel's guess, when Matthew asked in careful conversation at the pub one evening where Mary West might be. 'She does sometimes and stops over a day or two.'

'Not gone abroad, though?' Matthew asked, and at the answer, 'Not so far as I know,' felt an absurd and illogical relief that she was not that distant.

Jim was speaking to him. Matthew shook himself free from thoughts that had been burrowing in his head and heard Jim say that the country show was coming up soon, and why didn't he go and take that good little bitch of his.

'I know her leg's not altogether right yet, Matthew, but it's only a small course in the main ring: not like proper trials. Let her see what she can do.'

Matthew was puzzled: what was the man on about? He had not really been listening. Jim leaned across the bar and spoke again to Matthew, distinctly, as to a backward child.

'There's a competition for local sheepdogs at the county show. A sort of mini-trials, for local people to have a go at. I was saying you ought to take Jet.'

So that was it. Matthew glanced down at Jet lying at his feet and she raised her head from her paws and looked at him as if aware of the tenor of the conversation. She deserved the chance. She'd do well if he didn't let her down.

'I'll think about it,' he said.

And having thought about it, and committed himself, it seemed through some curious telescoping of time that he was almost at once there, on the show-ground, with no way out of it for himself or Jet. He must be mad. Neither of them had time for such foolishness. It was not even serious trial-work, just a bit of fun for the crowd. People jostled along the walks between cattle-rings and tractor-stands. There was a smell of crushed grass and hot canvas, with here and there a drifting suspicion of candy-floss and hot-dog with onions and hot engine-oil and steam from the roped-off area where stationary engines fussed and puttered, putting furious energy into doing abso-lutley nothing. A group of old men with faces as shining as boys' stood near the engines, with fingers that itched to touch them. They talked together, airing their knowledge of crankshaft and piston with every bit as much eagerness and assurance as the cocky young lads who waited to take their motor-bikes onto the dirt-track at the bottom of the field, with engines revving and buzzing like a nestful of hornets. It was as well the main ring was a fair distance from all of it. How could a dog keep its mind on its work with all this going on? Jet would need all her concentration, that was for sure.

The crowds thickened as the day wore on, and a steam organ began to churn the air with its hollow, brassy music. Mat-thew went to the beer-tent and consumed a sandwich he did not really want and a pint of mild that his stomach seemed none too happy with. He couldn't be nervous, surely? It was only a circus-act, just one more entertainment for the crowd. But he found himself shivering in spite of the heat of the day.

Soon it was time to move down to the main ring, where between the morning's cattle-show—which Matthew had eyed from a distance, thinking the pampered darlings not a patch on his own beasts—and the afternoon's show-jumping, the sheepdog competition was to take place. He recognized one or two local men with their dogs: Bert Hammond with his clever little tricolour bitch Fly, Martin Sims from the other side of Shepley, with a wall-eyed dog that was said to be good. Magpie would not be competing. She had picked up a wicked long thorn between the pads of her forepaw and was laid up at Pennant with an old sock on her foot.

The competition began and Matthew watched, appraisingly, the workmanship of each dog with its master: the style with which it handled the sheep; its temperament; above all, its relationship with the man it worked for. The standard was good but not brilliant, for it was only a small show, and there were enough mis-

244

takes to make the crowd laugh and keep their attention.

The competitor before Matthew was a shepherd from some miles away—Matthew did not know him—with a smooth-haired bitch, nearly white, with one pricked ear and one dropped. She started her work well enough, but as she drove the sheep between the hurdles, one grew skittish and broke away. She would have sent it back quick enough, but her master swore at her and she flinched and dropped, mistaking his anger for command. The sheep took advantage and soon it became obvious the white bitch had lost control of them as much as her master had lost control of his temper. She became snappish with panic as his impatience grew, and the sheep, as if to mock the pair of them, scattered among the crowd, behind trailers and horse-boxes, between parked cars. There was laughter from the crowd, which found the whole thing a huge joke, not appreciating the smarting disappointment of the shepherd frantically whistling his dog.

The sheep soon grew uneasy without each other's company, though, and gathered bleating together of their own free will behind the ice-cream stand, snatching at mouthfuls of grass to show they did not care, but panting for all that and unsure of themselves. The white bitch recovered her composure and got them back into the arena, where they trotted ahead, docile and obedient, to finish the course.

As soon as Jet began in her turn to work her sheep, Matthew knew she was going to be good. She ignored the crowd totally, as if she worked in such conditions every day. Her distance and pace were just right; she kept them going, yet with no suspicion of hurry; she was authoritative without being bossy. The crowd grew quiet to watch her, recognizing the quality of the dog, even though they did not all appreciate the finer points of what she was doing.

Then it was all over and Matthew and Jet turned to leave the ring. It was only at that moment that Matthew became properly aware of the great press of people that had stood watching them. Suddenly there was sweat on his forehead and he felt the old crushing awareness of too many people. He felt as he had done the first time his father had taken him to London, when he could only have been a handful of years old and had watched the crowds hurrying, purposeful as ants, but by no means as aware of each other. He had not shaken off that feeling of oppression until they were back home at Flint Hill.

Today, in the arena, with his old hat pulled down to shade his face and the work in hand to occupy him, he had felt fine; out there in that wide space with Jet and the sheep. But now he must walk back through this crowd, part them to let himself through, and because of Jet's good performance they were all looking at him, pressing forward, smiling and clapping. Matthew's head buzzed and he could not hear properly. The sound in his ears was like a great shore, ragged with seagulls, so that the crowd seemed at one and the same time pressed in on him and immeasurably distant. He was sweating enough to stick his shirt to his back now and yet something was making him shiver with cold under the blazing sun.

Somehow he found his way to the Landrover, Jet followed close at heel. She sprang to her accustomed place and he started up the engine. He was aware of people stepping back as he edged the vehicle out of its parking place. He thought he heard his name booming from the loudspeakers, but it could just as well have been from inside his head.

On the way home the road seemed to rise and fall beneath him, as if it moved rather than the vehicle. The steering column seemed unaccountably to have turned to jelly. Once or twice other traffic hooted and cars flashed their lights. He could not imagine why. If they chose to waltz about the road like that it was nothing to him.

It was not until he was back in the kitchen at Flint Hill that it occurred to him that he was ill. Great waves of shivering and nausea carried him into blackness.

Jet pawed at him anxiously as he lay on the stone floor and pushed him with her cold nose until he came to something like consciousness, enough at least to realize that he must get himself warm. He put more fuel on the kitchen fire and dragged the camp-bed alongside. All the while his body shook, and his head, which seemed in some way to have become detached from it, felt as though it were floating close to the ceiling like a balloon seeking escape.

When he had crawled onto the bed he felt a little better, though, and his head returned from its wanderings to rest on the pillow, where once established it seemed to wish never to be lifted again.

He dozed and shivered fitfully and his mind began to show him pictures of the day, very clear and yet distorted, like images in a convex mirror, so that he saw a huge and brilliant green field, with sheep moving like tiny clouds on a sky of grass and the people small and distant on the horizon. He watched the deft, clever manoeuvrings of the sheepdogs. He saw himself and Jet, and they floated easily about the field, and the sheep moved as one, their fleeces brilliant with sunshine, like the fleece that Jason went searching for among the islands of mythology.

Then, in a deeper dream, he was climbing high sheep-walks with Jet and a shadow-dog that might have been Trig but he could never see her quite clearly. Between them they gathered up sheep in their hundreds; thousands, perhaps; and now it was snowing and the wind was whirling it across from mountain-top to mountain-top, until distant sheep and flying flakes merged into one. He shook with the cold of it, but Jet was there, and the other dog, bunching the sheep, keeping them moving, and he must keep pace with them. And among all these fancies of his sleeping brain were pictures from his old bad dream, and he felt the hot harsh breath of flames, or was it the breath of that great grey dog, leaping to savage him? His body twitched in his sleep until these pictures faded.

Other dogs edged from memory into his dream, and scenes changed rapidly, disconcertingly. He saw old Gil, the collie of his baby days, and Seeker, Dan Ratton's retriever, who had never failed to find and fetch duck or partridge, grouse or hare, and who could swim like an otter. Matthew could smell in his dream the awful stink of the big yellow dog as he dried himself off in front of the fire after a hard day. Benjie was there too, Benjie who had come home from the hayfields in a thunderstorm, half demented with fear, and had led them back to Pete Jenner, his master, who lay struck dead by lightning in the middle of long Meadow. That had been the talk of Shepley for months.

Half waking, he considered these images he had seen and thought to himself of dogs that guard and fetch and find. Dogs to take the place of eyes. Dogs whose only job is to love the unlovable. His mind whirled again, confusing the images as if a kaleidoscope had been shaken in his head, and sometimes he saw Jet and sometimes Trig and sometimes any dog that had ever worked for any man. Then he was back again on that high mountain and the snow had trapped him and covered him like a stranded sheep, but Jet came and crawled in beside him and warmed him till he slept.

Later, he woke for a moment and wished that Jet were a St Bernard with a brandy-barrel around her neck. If he had brandy inside him he might manage to walk home through this snow. If only it weren't so cold. He dozed again, then opened his eyes and found he had woken, not into his dream but into reality, and the fire had gone out and it was almost dark.

The room was not really cold—it was a summer evening, after all—but to Matthew it seemed chilly, though Jet lay full-length against him and gave him all the warmth of her body.

He lay and thought that perhaps he should light the fire again, but none of his muscles seemed to want to move his bones to the task and his mind felt that the effort was too great. He closed his eyes and fell into a great pit of sleep, and this time he did not dream.

When daylight came, Jet nosed at him, puzzled. It was time for milking and she had never before known him not to wake for it, but he only stirred slightly and moaned in his sleep. She went to the door, anxious to be about her job of bringing the cows in, but it was shut and she had no way of opening it, so having scratched at it a little and whined, and padded up and down, she returned to her master and lay down by him as before.

Outside in the grey fields the cows called out with growing impatience, but no one came. The sun rose well above the horizon and still no one came. Old Blossom felt the swell of her udder grown hard against her legs and she bellowed her disapproval. In the kitchen, in response to the old cow's misery and worried by her master's stillness, Jet threw back her head and howled.

CHAPTER 16

Matthew woke to the feeling of warmth on his face. He opened his eyes and through the bleariness of them familiar objects swam up to be recognized: the big deal table; the black corner-cupboard; the stone window-seat with its usual clutter. Strangely, the fire was alight and the old kettle that squatted over it had steam at its lip and was murmuring quietly to itself.

It was very bright in the room. The sun was very high.

'God!' Matthew called out, and sat up so suddenly that the world spun. 'God! I've got to milk the cows!'

'John Davey has milked the cows,' said a voice, and a person stood in the sunlight between him and the window, a black silhouette against the bright radiance. But Matthew's eyes were not so dazzled that he did not instantly recognize her, and Jet, who was lying curled up beside him, raised her head at the sound of the voice.

Matthew lay back again, grateful to support his head on the pillow, and looked at Mary West who was carrying cups and plates from the sink to the table.

'I think I am about to ask a stupid question,' he said, carefully, finding that his throat hurt no less than his head. 'Like, what the hell are you doing, and how did you get here?'

'That's two questions,' Mary said. 'What I am doing is making you a hot drink. How I got here was on my own two feet.'

There was something wrong about that. She was supposed to be in Holton. She wouldn't have walked from Holton. Didn't sound likely at all.

'Thought you were in Holton,' he said, frowning.

'Don't look so puzzled,' she smiled at him. 'I was there until a couple of days ago and I've been busy whitewashing the kitchen since then, which is why I look leprous.' She pointed to splashes of white on her arms. 'I got so fed up with the smell of the stuff that I got up early this morning and went out walking in the woods. Then I heard your cows bellowing blue murder so I knew something must be amiss. Well, I'd turned Laurel out in one of the far fields, so I didn't waste time going to fetch him, I just legged it up the hill to find out for myself. I'm a real elephant's child, you know. Full of insatiable curiosity. Anyway, when I got as far as the yard gate I met John Davey coming up from Pennant on the same errand, and we both came in here and found you, with Jet stretched across you like something out of one of the old stories, daring the world to touch you. Luckily she had the sense to realize we'd come to help and she let me attend to you while Mr Davey went to see to the stock. He was in here a moment ago to say all was well and now he's gone back down to Pennant to phone Dr Sands.'

'No need for that,' Matthew said. 'It'll pass.'

'It's done now and you'll have to put up with it,' Mary said. 'It looks to me as if you've picked up some nasty virus.'

'But I'm never ill,' Matthew protested, against the evidence of his throbbing head and throat.

'All in the mind, is it?' said Mary, quizzically. 'You dislike what you fancy you feel then, I bet. Not much exposed to infection, are you, in the ordinary way? John Davey told me you went off to the show yesterday. Well, in that crowd there must have been some little bug that said, "Goody goody, no resistance!" and jumped on you with hobnailed boots.'

Matthew sat up, slowly, supporting his head on his hands, wincing at the painful accuracy of her description.

'I'll stay on my own hillside in future,' he groaned, 'and keep well clear of crowds.'

Mary gave him a mug of hot, clear

soup. It seemed an odd thing to start the day with, but he could sip it down easily, and the clean salt taste of it did not worry his throat. Then she poured some over hunks of brown bread which she had put on a dish for Jet, who tackled the meal gratefully. Matthew had been too ill to feed her when they came home from the show and she had eaten little the previous day. She stayed away from her master only long enough to polish the plate though, and then she was back alongside, relieved to see that he was more himself again.

Mary moved quietly about the room, making Matthew comfortable, putting things within reach, but she tidied nothing away, neither did she make any move to suggest that he should have his bed anywhere but where it was. Gradually it filtered into his mind that it was a pleasure to have her there, to watch her moving about. Illness had taken the lust from him, leaving this other curious pleasure in its place. Damn her, he'd missed the sight of her these last weeks, riding about his hillside. Well, he'd had a sense of something lost to him, that he wouldn't admit to.

'Dr Sands will come up after surgery, I expect,' she said. 'I'll stay till then.'

'If he's coming, would you like me to lie to attention and keep the covers tidy? Isn't that what nurses expect of their patients?' he said. Every word was an effort.

'Shall I pour a bottle of Dettol over you, to give the right atmosphere?' Mary suggested. 'You've some funny ideas about nurses, it seems, Matthew Ratton, and some very strange notions about me in particular. If you had seen my last hospital ward you might think differently.'

'Tell me,' he said.

She pulled the kitchen chair up by the fire, for the morning was still cool, despite the sunshine, with a wind blowing up the valley to take the warmth out of it. She slipped off her shoes and held her feet out to the fire, first one, then the other.

She has beautiful feet, Matthew thought.

'Tell me,' he said again.

She began to tell him about her time in Kandara and how she had worked in a ward made mostly of corrugated iron and packing cases, mortared mud and thatched overall with leaves and branches to keep off the sun, which on a tin roof would have roasted them as efficiently as a Dutch oven.

'It seemed to attract the lizards from all round,' she told him.

'How did you get rid of them?' he asked.

'Oh, I didn't get rid of them. They ate the flies.'

'What you'd call practical nursing,' Matthew said.

'Exactly,' she agreed. She told him about the people she had nursed, the women with their frail babies, the weaned children, big-bellied from their inadequate diet.

'They stand a chance while they're still on the breast, you see, but once there's another child to feed, the toddlers might as well eat glue for all the nourishment they get.'

She told him of the odd characters she had met from time to time, of how each day she learned to adapt her nursing to the people who needed it, so that they would accept treatment instead of avoiding it like the plague.

'We got one old man to come in for an operation,' she said, 'who wouldn't agree to it at all unless he could bring his three grandchildren and his goat with him.'

'Didn't anyone else mind?' Matthew asked.

'Why should they? The children ran errands and it was a fine goat.'

Matthew glanced out of the window to where his own Bella grazed on the bank. Mary saw where he was looking and she laughed.

'She's quite content where she is. And anyway, this old chap was convinced his goat was the reincarnation of his paternal grandmother. I assume you don't make that claim for yours?'

Matthew assured her that he did not. It was very comfortable by the fire and he felt a great sense of relief that Mary seemed entirely to have forgotten the animosity of their last encounter. She was obviously not a woman to bear a grudge, though he had given her plenty of cause. Well, he would not think about that now. He felt as weak as a half-drowned cat and childishly content to be watched over by her.

He must have dozed a little then, for he was presently aware of two voices, and there was Dr Sands, thermometer at the ready, asking him what he thought he'd been up to this time.

'I'll go back to the whitewash then,' Mary said. 'Peggy Davey will be up later.'

'Come tomorrow,' Matthew said. It was neither question nor command, but he knew she would come.

'Didn't really need that,' Sands said, shaking the thermometer at him. 'Obvious pyrexia. Throat hurts, doesn't it?

You'll just have to stay in bed and sweat it out. Take aspirin if you like. Those two women'll look after you, I don't doubt. And this one, too,' he added, prodding Jet with his finger.

'I feel awful,' Matthew said. 'I swear I'll never go near crowds again.'

'Nonsense,' said Sands, briskly. 'Now you've started making voyages among the human race again, you're not going to give up after one setback, are you? What if Columbus had said he thought he'd rather not look for a way round the world in case he picked up some nasty foreign disease? Anyway, it wouldn't be fair on Jet. John Davey tells me the talk in the pub last night was that she'd have won if you hadn't gone off before the finish. The last dog, the one after you and Jet, made a right mess of it apparently: sheep wouldn't do a thing right for him. You had the highest points of the lot, but they disqualified you because you'd left the field before the final announcement.'

'Damn me,' said Matthew.

'Well, give her another chance man, when you're fit again. Mary says the good little bitch was doing her best to play nursemaid to you and keep you warm last night, and wouldn't budge from you this morning, not even to stop Mag from coming onto her territory—all dot and carry one on three good legs— to take over your cattle when John Davey came up for the milking.'

'You seem to know a fair lot about what goes on,' Matthew said.

'Ears open, mouth shut,' said Sands.

'Not so's you'd notice, not the least bit,' Matthew commented. 'How long am I to be stuck here then?'

'A few days'll see you right.' The doctor washed his hands at the sink, collected his bag and went to the door. He opened it, letting in sweet summer air. The wind had dropped now.

'Here's Peggy Davey coming,' he told Matthew. 'I'll be off and leave her to it.'

For two days Matthew was so ill he was content to lie quietly in his kitchen, while the two women came and went, attending to him, and John Davey saw to the stock. Matthew found he could not even resent his helplessness; he had neither the will nor the energy. As for Jet, with a dog's wisdom she accepted this turn of events, this indoor existence that was so unlike her master. She stayed beside him and would only consent to go outside when one of the women escorted her round the garden.

On the third day he felt better enough to be irritable and Peggy Davey scolded him as if he were still in short trousers. He needed to be up now. John was a busy man, with his harvest to finish. He could not go on doing the Flint Hill work as well. Peggy would not hear of any such nonsense.

Matthew was still fretting when Mary came up later. He made as if to get out of bed, but Jet was lying across his legs and hampered him.

'Get down, you silly bitch,' he said, brusquely, and she looked up at him under her brows and thumped her tail, but for once did not obey him.

'Well now,' said Mary. 'You still don't know how to take help when it's offered, do you? She's been watching over you for days, and keeping you warm, as much as though she knew that's what you most needed, and what does she get for it? "Get down, you silly bitch!" Perhaps you'd like to tell me, "Go home, you silly bitch". Is that it?' She made the remark lightly, with no malice, but it got under Matthew's guard and brought him up short, aware of his surliness, both now and on previous encounters.

'I'm sorry,' he said and it was for more than his impatience with the dog.

Mary came across and sat down on the rag rug by the side of the bed and looked at him for a while. Then she took his hand.

'You are the only man I know,' she said, 'who could make those words sufficient: no explanation, no amplification. No need, because I know you mean them. You are forgiven.'

She set food ready for him and took Jet out into the air for a while. Then she came back, bringing the smell of outside with her. It was like the fragrance of baskets of clean laundry that his mother used to bring in from the garden. It was one of his few pictorial memories of her, slender and bare-armed, with her dark hair blown free of its pins by the same wind that had tugged the white sheets billowing on the line. It was a good smell.

'I'm off home now, Matthew,' Mary said, and she walked lightly to the door and was gone before Matthew had time to say a word. He lay and watched the door that had closed behind her and cursed its opaque solidity. He wanted to hold the sight of her in his eyes for a while yet. He stared so long and lay so still that at last Jet pushed against him with her nose and he seized her and cradled her to him as he had not done since she was a pup. In his mind's eye he saw Mary walking down to Tally Cottage and at last he let himself put a name to the feeling that he had for her. It was as if he were a child for whom the puzzling, angular symbols had at last resolved themselves into words, and he recognized love for what it was. He was not sure even now that he wished to admit it. Jet had been sufficient affection and companionship for him since the day he had found her on the dung heap and with her he had discovered a fine balance of content that satisfied them both. Yet still there flowed into his mind like rising water the fact that he loved Mary West and that somehow he must bring himself to tell her so, let her take it as she would.

On Peggy's next visit she found him much improved but still tetchy and very restless, as though something were eating him up. She had not seen him so ill as he had been these past few days since she had sat up with him in his childhood fevers. In her eyes it had stripped the years from him and she had enjoyed cossetting him as if he were a boy again, bringing special treats to tempt his appetite and books to keep him occupied.

Today she had brought him something different: a drawing-block and some pencils. He probably had plenty around somewhere but she doubted he'd know where to put his hands on them in that great muddle of a house. It wanted setting to rights and that was a fact. Her fingers itched to do it.

Matthew was pleased with his gift. He soothed his mind, making pencil-patterns on the white paper that gradually began to form intricate designs of leaves and animals all intertwined and interlaced, with jaws and stems and tails and tendrils mingled and mazed. When Peggy left he was concentrating so hard he was hardly aware of her going. She sighed as she walked down the path. They had been close again, the two of them, just for a moment, but it would not last. She knew, even if he did not, where he was going, but it was not her business to tell him. Perhaps he did know? She felt saddened by this old pain that she thought she had cured long since. God knew how she would be feeling if he were truly her son. Her own mother had said that children were never given you, only lent. Well, paying back was never easy. One always needed to ask for just a little more time.

In the Flint Hill kitchen there were drawings scattered all over the place: the elaborate patterns he had started with, drawings of sheep, studies of Jet from every possible angle, sketches of the views from the kitchen window. Mary looked at them carefully for a long time, considering their detail, their accuracy. Matthew had fallen asleep, the pencil still in his hand, and beneath his outflung arm was a drawing of her own face. She withdrew it with the utmost care so as not to wake him, and having looked at it a while, replaced it carefully so that he would not know she had seen it. Then she clattered about a little, to wake him up.

'You've been busy,' she said, when his eyes opened. As she suspected he would, he quickly gathered up the drawing of her.

'Have you been looking at them?' he asked.

'Some of them. Do you mind?'

'No.'

'Have you any others I could see?'

Matthew pointed to the chest of drawers in the far corner of the kitchen. 'Plenty in there,' he said.

Mary walked over to the chest and took out several folders of drawings. One contained studies of birds, another of trees and plants. She turned over page after page.

'They'd be just right,' she said. Her face was full of such obvious pleasure in the drawings that Matthew could not feel diffident about them as he usually did if anyone ventured to remark on them.

'Right for what?' he asked.

Mary came over and sat by him. 'Listen,' she said, 'in all the time I've been nursing in places like Kandara I've been keeping notes on anything I have found useful—all sorts of odd bits of information on anything from which insects will sting you to how to keep chickens out of the ward, what endemic diseases to watch out for, whether the local snakes bite or squash, the best way to persuade particular tribes to come for treatment when they can't see the reason for it. I told you I was an elephant's child, didn't I? I wrote down all sorts of stuff, just for my own benefit, but then one of our surgeons happened to see one of my notebooks and he's suggested I should make a book out of them to help the new nurses that come out, all fresh to the work and expecting St Thomas's Hospital, only hotter. He's got a brother-in-law who's in publishing and he's agreed to help, so I'm landed with the job.'

'Well?' said Matthew.

'It needs illustrating,' she explained. 'Drawings, your sort of drawings are just what it needs. I've got photographs, plenty of them, and slides and specimens and rough sketches I've done from time to time, so there'd be plenty to work from, but drawings throughout would give it a unity, rescue it from being a hotch-potch of information. Would you do it?'

Matthew looked at her uncertainly. 'What sort of things would you want drawn?'

She laughed. 'Bugs, bacilli, broken bones, poisonous plants, useful knots for tying up recalcitrant goats, maps of certain areas, plans of wards, theatre layout. It wouldn't be dull.'

He smiled back at her then, pleased that she should be so anxious for him to do this. He saw under his pencil-point, on the blank paper, exotic plants and coiled snakes and beautiful, kaleidoscopic patterns of microscopic life. Yes, he would do it.

'You have had quite a time of it, haven't you,' he said, 'while I have been working out my days at Flint Hill?' He looked at her, considering her slender hands, remembering her naked feet as she had held them out to the fire just those few days ago. He saw the depth there was to her eyes. Funny that some eyes are shallow and reflect away the glance of the one that looks at them. These of hers had seen many things that perhaps, once, he might have longed to see, and also, more likely, a good deal that he would have no wish ever to see.

'My world has been much smaller than yours, all my life,' he said. 'This place is all I know and for the most part I'm content with it. If you want me to draw these exotic things you'll have to teach me about them. To put it bluntly, I'm a bit of a dull fellow, but perhaps I could earn a little salvation by drawing your beasties for you.'

There were other things he must say too, but she looked so delighted he dared not risk spoiling that.

'Thank you, Matthew. Thank you. Now when I come back in the New Year I can settle to the book and get it done.'

There was a long pause. Jet, asleep at the foot of the bed twitched a little in dreams and sighed.

'You never told me you were going,' Matthew said. Of course he had known she would be going. He just had not let himself think about it. 'When?'

'In a day or so. I'll be back. And then it will be for good. This is my last tour of duty and then I take up a post at Clipton

Hospital.'

'Won't you find that dull?'

'No,' she said. She was amused that he asked the question with careful politeness while his mind was holding on with such obvious pleasure to the fact that next time she would not be going away again. He really did not know, did he, how transparent he was.

'It'll be different,' she said, 'but not dull. It's like what you were saying about your being here all these years while I've been gadding about. You can only live under one patch of sky at a time and the glamour of being somewhere else usually lies in the fact that it's distant from reality. When you are actually there, it *becomes* reality and the glamour lies in a yet more distant place. Am I talking nonsense?'

'No,' Matthew said. 'It's the best of sense.'

He gathered up the drawings from the bed and stuffed them together into a bundle and set them aside. He brushed away some imaginary crumbs from the blanket. He linked his arms around his knees and hooked his fingers around each other, making a tight shape of himself, as if to resist a blow, and then he spoke.

'Could you like me a little, do you think?'

She had been looking at Jet. Now she turned her face to him. Knowing what she knew of herself, what was she to say to that? He did not wait for an answer though, but went on, talking to his hunched knees, as if not to look at her would prevent her wrong reply.

'I'm a God-awful sight, I know, but you must be used to worse than me. I've no words of love to speak better than the ones I throw to my dog, but I've got to tell you that I love you, because that's the truth.'

With the greatest of effort he raised his head to look at her and was entirely surprised by the answer he saw there. Mary put out her hand and gently and deliberately touched the ridges of skin on the maimed side of his face. There was something beyond affection in the gesture: it was a courteous, compassionate acceptance of his disfigurement that almost overwhelmed him. He had thought that never again without flinching could he bear anyone to touch his face, but now he put his hand on hers and held it there. It was an action more intimate than any more directly sexual one and held far more of a commitment in it.

They sat, so, without words, until Jet, puzzled by their stillness, put an imperative paw between them. Mary glanced down and spoke to her, 'Well, Jet, are you worried that I'm taking your man's attention from you?'

The collie waved her tail and laid her ears flat to her head. She was aware of the currents that passed between these two and was puzzled, but not alarmed. What was good for her master she would accept for herself, unless she were forbidden, and there was no rejection in the air. It all smelt right.

Mary was speaking again and she rubbed Jet's ears gently as she addressed her.

'You see, Jet, if you consider the infinite nature of love, you will not find it surprising that mine can easily extend to one man and his dog. And will yours stretch a little to accept me, do you think?'

Jet liked the sound of the words. Soothed by them, she lay down quietly, head on paws. Soon she was asleep, leaving the two to their own company.

CHAPTER 17

'Have you seen to the Flint Hill beasts, John?'

Peggy Davey called across to her husband where he sat on the high seat of the old Ford tractor. Young Steven, Ellen's boy, had helped him strip it down over the weekend, but it still made enough noise for the whole Ford works put together. Once he started that engine you could shout till your lungs burst and he'd never hear you, what with the noise of the machinery and the thickness of the ear-muffs that he wore. One day they'd buy a modern monster with air-conditioning and a sound-proof cab. That would be the day. The old, blue, mechanical work-horse had not started its clatter yet, though, so he was able to hear her.

'I'm not needed, it seems,' he shouted

back. 'Young Matthew was up on his feet when I called last night. Said he'd walked about the place a bit and he'd be all right. I went up just now and I heard the cooler running, so I left him to it.'

'Are you sure he'll be all right?' Peggy came across the yard and looked up into the tractor cab, her face concerned. Davey leaned down and patted her affectionately.

'Don't *fuss,* woman,' he said.

'I'll go up later,' said Peggy. 'Just to be sure.'

'Well, make it this afternoon then, my love. Mary's going up this morning, to say goodbye. She's got a plane to catch.'

'Off so soon? It doesn't seem a moment since she came home. Well, he's going to miss her. It seems to me he's come to his senses at last where she's concerned.'

'She's been up there often enough, and that's a fact, since he took ill,' John Davey agreed.

'Yes,' said Peggy. She stood a while, turning her foot from side to side in the dusty gravel of the yard.

'You're looking thoughtful, lass,' her husband said.

'I was only thinking about Matthew. Hoping he'll be happy.'

'Aye, and wondering what the two of them have been up to together, with her so much in his company at Flint Hill every day?'

He was laughing at her. She went pink and her eyes flashed annoyance at him. She felt as ruffled as an old hen and cross with herself for feeling so.

'John! I wasn't!' she exclaimed. 'It's no one's business but their own what they do. I'm just pleased to see the life come back into him.'

'And a mite jealous that another woman did it. Admit it now!' he teased.

'And why should I be jealous,' she countered, 'when I have a man of my own, even if he is wearing a bit thin in places? And a bit fat in others. Now, I've no more time to stand here listening to your nonsense and getting nothing but a crick in my neck for my trouble. Start that engine and be off with you.'

She stumped away, her husband's chuckling drowned by the sudden eruption of the motor. The tractor chugged out of the yard. She smiled to herself now, her annoyance gone. John was right, of course. She was finding it hard to give Matthew up to someone else, however right for him, however much she had seen the rightness of it from the beginning. Her relationship with Matthew, from his childhood, had been lightly held, seldom referred to, and perhaps he would never know how dear he was to her. She drew herself up determined to be glad for him. After all, it was she herself who had said it would be the best possible thing. Of course it was.

Matthew was at the Flint Hill gate, looking down the valley, relishing the air on his face. It had been so good to get out again. Since his first shaky tour of the garden, with Mary's arm about him and Jet going mad with delight, rushing about the grass and rolling and rubbing her ears on the ground in an ecstasy of freedom, he had felt his energy return slowly to him like sap rising in a tree. Now he was waiting for Mary to come and his pleasure was tinged with the melancholy thought of her leaving him for so long. These last two days they had walked the farm together, so far as Matthew's legs could yet take him, and he had shown her his land and told her his plans for it, and she had watched Jet work the sheep and had helped at the milking. How could he ever have thought her anything but just the right woman for him? Whatever she did about the place, she looked right and proper doing it. What he had imagined in his early days to be love had been an oyster—all grit and no pearl. What was that trite phrase? 'This was the real thing.' Well, my God, so she was. His real thing, and now he knew her worth and now she was coming to say goodbye. In the distance he could see her.

'Come, Jet,' he said and they set off down the track to bring her home to Flint Hill.

It was as well there was plenty ahead to be done. The year was flourishing now, and there was the harvest to finish and store. It had been a fair summer and they had been able to make an early start on the grain harvest. New stock was growing visibly, plumped by the last flush of summer grass. It was coming up time for tupping, so there was work to be done checking over the ewes, making sure all were fit and well. Matthew had kept back a couple of his own ram lambs to use on the hill flock, and he had culled the poor-looking tups that he had found running there. They were not worth the extra rations. He was glad of the work to be done and glad of his recovered strength. He appreciated the growing fitness of his body after having had to lie like a felled tree for what had seemed to him so long. And fit he was again in a very short time, fit in the proper sense of apt for the job. He remembered Miss Atherly urging him to take pride and pleasure in his skills. Well, so he would. And he'd take Jet to the area trials too. She was working better than ever, with all trace of her limp gone. It seemed to him that she knew his mind, could almost anticipate his thought. He felt she could make sheep jump through hoops if he asked her.

They walked up one evening to the Tally flock and he sent her to gather a small bunch of ewes that were grazing near the quarry. He looked them over and found no problems. They would be fit enough for tupping: a sight better than they had been a year ago. It would take a good many seasons to build a fine flock here though, for that was a thing you could not hurry. He hoped Jet would be there to see it and he wished her span were longer. 'Work, time and a bit of luck, that's what we need, my girl,' he said to her.

The September air cooled a little as cloud-shadows came drifting over the hill, making alternate patches of dark and light that shifted and moved with the breeze. Flint Hill lay below, first in sun, then in gloom and then in sun again. Matthew looked along the boundaries of of his land, studying each field that lay alongside, glad to see them in good heart, and he checked in his head the rotation for the following year.

He set off down the hill, calling Jet off the ewes who ambled away, grazing as they went, back to the particular pasture they had chosen for that evening, the sweet grass at the quarry's edge. They were in no danger there, for they were canny creatures and knew their territory like their own forefeet.

Matthew had not intended to go down to the cottage, but somehow he found himself there. He stood in the overgrown garden with Jet pressed against his leg and in the sheltered valley the evening was windless. A bird sang in the orchard, its music mellow and golden yet with a cleansing sharpness to it, tart as the yellow windfall plums that lay scattered in the grass. Matthew stood there, looking at the odd little house among the trees, and he thought about Mary and felt as foolish as a schoolboy for doing it. He wanted it to be New Year, with smoke drifting from the empty chimney that now rose up before him. He laughed at himself and began to wander aimlessly about the orchard. He came to an old tree with a broad trunk to it and he leaned his back against it, buckling his legs slowly so that he slid downwards to sit angled against the tree. Little ridges and unevennesses of bark pressed into his spine and shoulder-blades so that he had to ease himself into a comfortable position. There were apples on the down-hung branches of the tree and some on the ground. He found one that the wasps had not yet discovered. It was a small, sweet fruit of the sort they call summer apples, that can be eaten while the Laxton and the Cox and the James Grieves are still sour enough to curl your tongue. He bit into it and gave a piece to Jet, and they sat quite still under the tree and let the dusk close round them.

Matthew watched the surrounding trees lose their third dimension as the light faded, to become silhouettes against the sky. What angles their old branches made, what fine lacework in their top-most twigs. He wished he had his sketch-book with him, but then he could scarcely have seen the paper in the gloom, and a torch, lit to see by, would have blinded his eyes to the very thing he wanted to draw. He would have to carry the pattern of branches in his mind and put it to paper when he got home. He thought of the drawings he was to do for Mary and his fingers flexed as his mind set about deciding how best to tackle the job. Line, he thought: not too delicate, little shadow. Clarity was what was needed, so there could be no mistaking what each picture represented, in detail and with precision. Then he thought of Mary and what he had told her about his feelings for her and what countless things remained unsaid. He had been so amazed that she loved him that he had not dared to think beyond that and even now those further thoughts seemed imprecise and shadowy, with no clarity beyond the fact and declaration of their feelings for each other.

The air grew chilly and Matthew and Jet left the orchard and began their walk back to Flint Hill. The moon was up now, and down by Pennant, where some of the fields had been cut already and the straw bales carted from them, the stubble gleamed under its light. Bare, empty, ghosts of fields. Somewhere a fox barked and an owl, disturbed, floated past like a shadow of shadows. Small, familiar noises came from the woodland.

Matthew supposed that in Kandara the night air would be filled with more strident sounds, from alien creatures that he had never seen, that would make Jet's lip curl and her hackles rise. The worst she was likely to happen on here might be some short-tempered old boar-badger on his way home, blundering myopically through the undergrowth on one of his familiar tracks to the sett. Matthew was glad of his known world.

Then, in the distance, a dog howled in a long mournful crescendo, unsettled perhaps by the brightness of the moon. Matthew's skin prickled, remembering the grey sheep-killer. But that was nothing but old bones now under the turf of the field-ditch at Flint Hill. What a dog that had been: the savagery of it. He had felt a grudging admiration for the beast, even though it had damned near killed him. It had made the best, according to its instincts, of the bad deal man had given it. Thoughts of the grey dog and the chill of the night air made him shiver a little and quicken his pace. It must be close on midnight. Shepley would think him moon-struck, wandering about the countryside at this time of night, and him with cows to milk in the morning. Shepley would be, for the most part, asleep and snoring, except perhaps for one or two lads he knew of who might still be about after rabbit or pheasant in places they had no right to be.

He looked down at Jet, trotting at heel, her blackness almost swallowed up in the shadows. He called her name, softly, and she looked up. He saw the whiteness of her teeth and the tongue lolling across them in her familiar grin.

He supposed it was not a smile as a human smiles, but it was a pleased expression for all that.

'Good bitch,' Matthew said.

Before she left, Mary had extracted from Matthew his promise to take Jet to the area trials at Faverton, and word had got round, as it has a way of doing in villages, that the Flint Hill dog was entered. There was no way Shepley would let Matthew forget about it now, even if he wanted to. Jet's luck was drunk to at the Dog and Partridge, children asked after her on Matthew's rare walks to the village. The milk-tanker driver brought her a bone from his family's week-end joint. It was a good while since a Shepley dog had been entered at Faverton. Matthew did not know how to take this at all. He had thought it was his affair, his and Jet's, and now everyone's hopes seemed to be riding on her back, wanting her victory. He had to keep a hold of himself to stop the old panic come marching in again. It would be too much for Jet, the standards too high, the other competitors old hands at the game and well versed in it, while he could only ask his dog to do the job she always did and hope it was good enough for the judges. These feelings almost overset him altogether and it was only with an effort that he got himself away to Faverton on time on the day, forcing himself not to dawdle, not to delay, not to make excuses not to go.

On the way, Jet sensed his tension and instead of curling up in the back of the Landrover as she usually did, she sat bolt upright, ears erect, watching the unfamiliar landscape as they drove on.

They found the place easily enough. The ground was beautifully set out, with the sloping hillsides making a perfect place for spectators, overlooking the large arena in which the dogs would work. It was not easy land though, Matthew saw at once. The arena itself sloped quite steeply, from the little plateau at the top where the sheep would be loosed to the lonely white post on the lower ground where the shepherd must stand and wait for his partner to bring the flock down to him. Halfway down the slope was a long, straight depression in the ground, like a flat ditch, the last trace of an old cart-track perhaps, and a rough bridge of planks was set across it to form one of the obstacles of the course. There were the familiar hurdles and the cross-shaped passage of planks, the Maltese Cross through which the sheep must be driven and turned and driven again: there was the shedding ring, marked with white-painted stones, and there was the pen, the final goal, where each dog's five sheep must finish their run. Everyone and his dog was milling about the place, talking knowledgeably, looking at home and at ease. Matthew's heart went to his boots.

These were proper trials, not just a side-show, one of the 'many other attractions' that the competition at Clipton had been. Here, the whole day was dedicated to the shepherd and his dog and there were no distractions. Everyone who had come to watch was there for the sheer interest of seeing the men and the dogs working together, perhaps with the co-operation but more often the un-willing attention of the sheep.

As he and Jet moved about in this company, however, some of his panic began to subside. It was an atmosphere to which he felt attuned and although the company seemed to him exalted, he soon began to feel at home in it. In spite of the inevitable tension, the competitive edge to the occasion, he recognized in every-one about him a common interest, a unity of purpose, as in a theatre where a dedicated audience waits on a brilliant cast. He sat on the turf with Jet between his knees and listened to the sheep-talk, the snatches of conversation about the merits of that dog against this; about old So-and-so's bitch that nearly won up in Wales last week but the sheep broke at the pen and lost her the competition; how old Fly got such bad sheep a few weeks back he could hardly knock up any score at all; how Tom Mogg's bitch could pen sheep any day of the week but they wouldn't go up in that bloody trailer for her, no matter what.

Listening to them, it occurred to him again what professionals they were: he and Jet would have to have their wits about them. Jet was looking out over the landscape, relaxed but eager, watching the small figures of the sheep in the distance. She was something special, Matthew knew that. She quivered slightly under her glossy coat and her ears were alert. Silky hair hid the long scars on her body, but his fingers could feel them as he caressed her. Two of a kind, we are, he thought to himself. What was the phrase? Bloody but unbowed. As he scanned the crows, Matthew recognized one or two Shepley faces. So they'd come to watch him, had they? There were the Daveys and that young Sarah—come to stay with them a while. There'd been trouble at home, Matthew knew. Well, Peggy would sort that out, no doubt about that. He saw other familiar faces too and here and there a hand was raised in greeting, but no one came up to him.

They knew Matthew well enough to know he would want all his mind on the job in hand.

'We'll have a go, Jet, just see if we won't,' he said aloud, and Jet turned her head to him and grinned, as if she agreed with every word.

One after another the men and their dogs went down to the post. It looked the loneliest place in the world. Each dog had his fresh bunch of five sheep to gather and fetch, down the slope to the wooden bridge, over the bridge, between the hurdles and down to the post. At this point the dog's job changed from fetching the sheep to driving them and then he worked in closer partnership with his master, whereas before he had been, as it were, at remote control. The drive took the sheep between more hurdles and then through the Maltese Cross, first one way, turn and then the other. Then came the shedding ring where one sheep, marked with a ribbon, must be singled from her companions, and finally all five sheep must be safely penned between three hurdles with a gate across them. There was a length of rope attached to the gate so that the shepherd, with rope and crook, could baulk the sheep to one side and make the dog's work easier. And the skilful dogs and their handlers made it look easy, though even they could be caught out sometimes, by bad sheep or by the tiniest mistake in turning or in positioning themselves. On the farm it would not matter, they would soon have things right again, but here the points fell away for each small error as the judges watched, hawk-eyed, from their table.

One little tricolour bitch worked really well, Matthew thought, but she was old and getting slow and could not finish within the time. He saw her panting as she ran out to her sheep and he thought then that if Jet's lameness were going to make itself felt it would be on that punishing outrun.

There was one more dog to go now, before it was Jet's turn. Matthew once again felt the tension in himself and in the onlookers too, but theirs was excitement and his was apprehension. He wished himself anywhere but where he was, and his throat felt so dry he doubted he could call or whistle far enough for the keenest-eared dog to hear. He pulled at Jet's ear and she turned her head, to draw her tongue across his hand, once only, and then she fixed her attention again on what was happening around her. Her quick, consoling gesture moved him. He knelt down and drew her against him in rough affection. The hell with his nerves. He had got the best collie in the world here. He had watched some fine sheepwork that day: good dogs and skilled shepherds. It seemed to him there was little likelihood of matching them. But for all that, Jet was the best there was. She was last in the line, and Matthew had been glad of that, when he had seen the order of competing. At least when he had finished, do well or badly, it would be over and done with, with no one else to do better or worse after him.

The dog to work before Jet came

eagerly into the arena. He was a big, heavy dog, long-coated, prick-eared, moving with quick agility despite his size. He worked with a little wizened Welshman who could easily have been ninety years old but was every bit as active as his dog. As they began their work, Matthew could see that it was a good partnership, but there was something about the dog that Matthew did not like—a predatory eagerness which to Matthew's mind showed him to be too close to his original instincts, essential though those instincts were. With Jet, as it had been with Trig, the old lust of their ancestors had been channelled so that—in Matthew's opinion at least—they would no more have turned on the sheep than a skilled fencer would lunge with bare foil and impale his opponent. There were many who would not agree with him, he knew. Many shepherds would say that a dog worked well only because of its domination by man and needed little excuse to be at the throats of the sheep, but Matthew had watched Jet with the lambs, had seen her gentle along the ewes heavy with young, had seen with what care she drove the cows in when their udders were full and cumbersome, firm with their crankiness, but never rough. He would trust her anywhere.

The big dog was doing well in spite of Matthew's reservations and the points were high. He was obviously a well-known dog and there were noises of encouragement from among the crowd. Matthew's gloom descended on him again but he made himself go on watching, acknowledging the dog's skill. Then, when it came to the shedding ring, and the marked ewe was to be singled from her companions, the dog had a deal of trouble with her as she seemed determined not to be parted from them. Twice she managed to turn and huddle against her companions, instead of moving a clear distance away. She was a big ewe and not easily dominated, the sort that always makes trouble. Exasperated, he gave her a sharp nip as he came through to turn her and was rated soundly by his master for doing it. This upset the dog and he was slow to come up to his sheep to pen them, for all the world as if he were sulking, but the sheep went in, and the gate slapped to, just within the time allowed.

Matthew and Jet walked into the arena, to that lonely post that they had seen so many others approach. He took it deliberately slowly to calm himself down and to give Jet time to get her bearings. He could feel his heart thumping and when he got to the post he had to blink hard to focus his eyes and his mind on the distant sheep. The stopwatch would not start till he sent Jet off for the gather. From the post he could now see clearly the sheep waiting at the top of the field, nibbling unconcerned at the grass. A slight rise and fall of ground immediately in front of the post would mean that they were not in sight at all as far as Jet was concerned. Matthew pondered on the supreme optimism needed to send a dog into a vast expanse of seemingly empty field in the hope that it would return with five unknown sheep in some semblance of order. What dog but the collie would do it? None, and that's for sure, he thought.

Suddenly he was aware that his anxiety was gone. He was here now and there was a job to be done. He had best get on with it. He summed up the ground and decided that, as he had thought from the side-lines, a left-hand gather would take Jet up the slightly less steep side of the arena and save her leg a bit. 'Good bitch,' he said and gave her the office to go off to the left. He had put the crowd out of his mind now, and the strangeness of the place and the excitement of the day, so that nothing should matter but Jet and the sheep.

He watched her intently on the outrun and to his relief there was not the least hint of lameness as she covered the rough ground. She was up to her sheep now, lifting them quietly, bringing them down the steep slope at a steady pace. If they set off at a gallop down this hill you would be hard put to get them back again before they reached the next county. She got them to the bridge and they did not like it, the hollowness under their hoofs. Several dogs had had their sheep break here and go down the ditch instead, but Jet pressed on to them, showing her authority. Matthew thought she would lose a point or so for the hesitation, but they were well over now. She brought them dead centre between the hurdles and over the slight rise in the ground towards him. The biggest of the ewes—who, like the troublesome one the last dog had had, was the boss of the bunch to judge by her actions—was looking all the time as if she would like to give Jet trouble, but Jet had a weather eye on her, ready to forestall any bad move she might make.

Now they started their drive. The hurdles were easy enough, the turn not as tight as the judges might think correct, but a good straight cross-drive to make up for it. The sheep went meekly enough through the Maltese Cross and turned well and started to go through again, but then the bad ewe broke away and there was an 'Oh!' from the crowd. But Jet was there in a flash and crouched to her and she thought better of it and trotted demurely through. The pace had been good all the way through. Jet had kept them at a smart trot but they had not broken into a run. If they did not make the time it would be bad luck, but Matthew was not going to hurry sheep, even in the trials. He had seen one or two dogs galloping the flesh off them that afternoon and he wasn't having it, points or no points.

Matthew was glad it was not the bossy ewe who was marked for singling. He stood alongside the sheep with his eye on the ribboned one and waved his stick a little to spread them out. Jet waited, ready, and he called her on through. He could hear scattered clapping from the crowd. Jet held the ewe away from the rest for a moment or so and then let her rejoin the others for the penning. She had done well there, Matthew thought. Then he walked briskly to the pen and reached for the rope to set the gate open wide, holding his stick out at an oblique angle to make himself as long an obstruction to the sheep as possible. He hardly dared breathe as she brought the sheep up to him. If they broke now—! But she had no hint of trouble at the pen. The sheep went sweetly in and the gate shut. They were safe and home and well within the time. Well, between them they had not made a mess of it at any rate.

'That'll do, Jet,' Matthew said.

They walked back to the crowd's edge and sat down side by side on the grass. Matthew felt as tired as if he had worked a full day's harvesting. His legs were leaden and his eyes felt sore from the intensity of concentration. He closed them for a moment and bowed his head forward on his knees. It was amazingly quiet: so many people, and yet so still, all waiting. You could feel the expectancy, the hope: it was like electricity in the air.

Over at their table, the judges sat with heads bowed, totting up points. They deliberated, unhurried. It continued very

305

quiet all across the hillside. A runner was sent across to the loudspeaker van. There was a crackling and squeaking and the amplified clearing of a throat as the precursor to the announcement of the result. Then a familiar name boomed from the speaker and applause began to ripple through the crowd. A Shepley voice shouted, 'Good old Jet!' The applause grew louder and beat in Matthew's ears.

Matthew could not, for a full minute, comprehend that they had won, he and Jet, but they said it again, as if to reassure him. Then, suddenly, he felt such triumph that it could not be contained. He picked Jet up fore and aft and held her over his head as if he were lifting weights. He turned himself around to let the crowd see her, this fine dog of his, and his face—scars and all—could not hide his supreme pleasure.

The other shepherds—quiet men leading solitary, reticent lives, sparing of praise, niggardly of emotion, surprised though they might be at this reaction to a victory which for them would have called forth nothing more than a slow smile—looked at Matthew with his dog and saw that his triumph was more than the winning of the trials, and they stood and clapped him heartily.

Jet looked down at her master, more than a little amazed at being in this position. She knew she had pleased him though, so she put up with all the extraordinary business that seemed to go with her success with an equanimity sprung from her supreme trust in him.

Then, when it was all over and time to go back to Flint Hill, she trotted after Matthew to the Landrover and curled herself up in her usual place. The engine started and she muffled her nose with her tail and fell asleep.

MARY ANN GIBBS TITLES IN LARGE PRINT

The Romantic Frenchman

A Most Romantic City

The Moon in a Bucket

Wife for the Admiral

The Tempestuous Petticoat

A Young Lady of Fashion

ANNE HAMPSON TITLES IN LARGE PRINT

Song of the Waves

An Eagle Swooped

Stars over Sarawak

Reap the Whirlwind

DENISE ROBINS TITLES IN LARGE PRINT